Jace

The moment was fraught with intimacy

April nuzzled Jace's broad shoulder, loving the texture and scent of him.

"You remind me of a puppy, the way you do that," he said huskily. One hand spanned her waist and slowly moved up to her swelling breast.

"And you remind me of a big hound," April murmured, feeling her body turning to warm honeyed liquid. "Five-foot-five women aren't supposed to date six-foot-three men. It's in the law books."

Jace nibbled on her earlobe. "You don't date me. You share my life and my bed. And," he whispered teasingly, "you match me very well when we're lying down...."

THE AUTHOR

Rita Clay Estrada lives in Texas with her husband, James, and four children. Now a full-time writer, Rita previously worked as a secretary, cosmetics saleswoman and bookstore manager.

This prolific author, whose pen names include Rita Clay and Tira Lacy, firmly believes romance is here to stay. "Love may not make the world go 'round," she asserts, "but it's certainly the magic ingredient that makes it all worthwhile."

The Will and the Way

RITA CLAY ESTRADA

Harlequin Books

TORONTO • NEW YORK • LONDON
AMSTERDAM • PARIS • SYDNEY • HAMBURG
STOCKHOLM • ATHENS • TOKYO • MILAN

This one is for...

Pam Zollman, my teacher and friend.
She's sunshine and laughter on stormy days....
And
Tate McKenna, who knew me before,
during and after and has always
been there when I needed her.
Bring on the margaritas!

Published February 1985

ISBN 0-373-25148-3

1

"CAN YOU HONESTLY CONDEMN my client just because he took the word of those from whom he buys?" Ringing with justice, April Flynn's low, firm voice filled the Monday-morning air of the courtroom. "He was just as cheated by those he worked with as the home buyers for whom he was working. The fault here lies with the subcontractors, who provided slipshod merchandise and workmanship, not with my client."

Jace Sullivan stood in the back of the room and watched Flynn as she tried to sway the jury to her client's side. He should have already been at the meeting with Sid, his agent, but as he passed the courthouse he remembered that April was pleading a case this morning. He couldn't resist the pull that led him to the parking lot and into the courtroom to watch her, if only for a few moments. He also couldn't help the prideful grin that etched his mouth. She was magnificent. Her short-cropped dark-brown hair framed her face and showed off her slim neck and high cheekbones. Her figure was divine, right down to her long, slender legs. Her eyes, though, were her best feature. They were a brilliant blue when she was angry and soft, silky blue-gray when she was making love.

Not only was she good-looking enough to capture a

third and fourth glance, she was also intelligent and witty, a challenge to his own way of thinking. And she was terribly sexy voiced. He could already feel her voice stirring him into thoughts best left to the privacy of their home.

"Their" home. It was actually "his" home. She had moved in, after much cajoling, a little over three years ago. He hadn't regretted one moment of her being with him. In fact, it seemed like the most natural thing in the world. Before Jace had met her, he had gone through a series of affairs, one running into another until he couldn't begin to tell the next blonde from the first brunette. He had never belonged, really belonged, to any woman until April Flynn had walked into his life and his heart.

She had broken every rule he'd set for himself in a relationship. She worked hard, argued, didn't cook or clean, demanded that civilized manners be shown at all times. In short, she forced him to behave the way he'd sworn he'd never behave for another woman. She was a career woman, anything but docile and demanded equality in every facet of their relationship, from lovemaking to dirty dishes. And he loved it.

They belonged together. He couldn't begin to imagine what it would be like if she weren't there. She made his days bearable and his nights wonderful. . . .

His heart thumped heavily in his chest, warning him to get off that idea. She was his and that was that. She wasn't going anywhere. She was going to stay with him for the rest of her life. He'd make sure of that.

With something akin to awe and wonder, he realized what he had just been thinking. It wasn't the first time marriage had been on his mind. It had been popping up at the most inopportune moments for the past three months. Was he crazy? Yes and no. He had always given every excuse in the world for not getting married, including his fear of repeating his first marriage. That had been a mistake. But he had only been nineteen at the time. Young and stupid and "in love" was what he had been, although he'd been too blind to see himself that way until April stepped into his life. The marriage had lasted for one hellish year, and then they'd parted—not so amicably.

But the plain fact was that he'd never committed himself to, never been involved with anyone else. Until Flynn he had been a loner.

He was thirty-six now, and his first marriage was a long time ago. It hadn't hurt his heart, and it didn't hurt his ego to think of that past mistake any more. He grinned. His relationship with Flynn was in no way like that union.

He stood straighter, his brown eyes narrowing as he watched her. Her hands moved in graceful unison to her words and steps, reminding him of an accomplished geisha.

It was time to make a public commitment. To Flynn.

He relaxed slightly as he remembered the vacation they had been planning all year. It wasn't easy to correspond time-off so both of them could get away together. They had rented a cabin in upper Oregon. For one month they wouldn't do anything they didn't want to do. There was no phone, no TV, and there were no people. It would be a perfect, idyllic retreat.

In fact, it'd be the perfect place to propose. Then, after spending three weeks at the cabin, they'd leave a week early and fly to Reno, where they could be married before returning to L.A. and buckling down to work. He had a movie contract to begin then, and he knew she would want to get back to her practice. It was ideal timing. He had five weeks to get her ready for the most romantic month of her life.

Jace smiled smugly. His eyes never left Flynn's face. When she turned, with all her decorum and grace present, to bend over the desk and reach for one of her papers, she gave him a sexy, sly wink. He winked back.

A woman in the back row began pointing to him and talking to her neighbor. They both smiled and waved as if they had known him forever. He smiled distantly and nodded in acknowledgment, then glanced at his narrow-banded gold watch and noted the time. He had better leave before they asked for his autograph.

Once more his thoughts turned to Flynn. Marriage still felt right. Assured that his decision was a sound one, he hurried quietly out the courtroom door.

Later this evening he would begin wearing Flynn down so she would be ready for his proposal and accept, instead of bucking him. He'd stop acting like a husband, a routine he had slipped into naturally, and begin acting more like a lover. He'd sweep her off her feet and carry her away on pink clouds of romance. He grinned again. That wouldn't be hard; she had the ability to turn him into the world's greatest Casanova with just the one right glance. And that was no acting; that was real.

But right now it was time to meet with his agent.

APRIL FLYNN SLIPPED HER SHOES OFF and pushed them to the side of her leather swivel chair. Her desk held a million sheets of paper, most needing to be read and given a simple yes or no. Her paralegal and friend, Sam, could have handled most of them himself, but April liked knowing what was going on in her office. Besides, it was good training for her to go over these points with him, since he was going to be her partner as soon as he completed law school.

She leaned back and closed her eyes, giving a grunt to the knock on the office door. Opening one eye, she watched Sam walk to the cabinet and fix two perfectly chilled margaritas, then walk back to stand in front of her.

"Drink," Sam ordered, his usually raspy voice even rougher in command.

And April did, slowly but with thorough enjoyment. The drink was just what she needed as she pondered her problem. "Mmm, thanks, Sam. If you could fix the rest of my problems with such a quick solution, you'd have job security forever."

Sam chuckled, a deep throaty sound that soothed sore nerves, as he sprawled in the chair across from her. His dark-brown hair took on russet tones as the fluorescent light bounced off its vibrancy. His brown eyes twinkled with his ever-present good humor. "Well, then, give me a try. If it doesn't have to do with the case you're on now, I may be able to help."

"What's wrong with the case I'm on now?" She sipped again, licking greedily at the salty rim that paradoxically eased her dry throat.

"Because I think those poor suckers who bought those houses couldn't have known to check a septic system before they moved in. The builder was the person who should have checked the work. He's also the one who should have checked the building-code requirements for that part of town. Instead he wants to knock the home buyers into big bucks getting it fixed." Sam had faced a similar problem once with his duplex, and April had realized it in time to make sure he did none of the follow-up on this case.

"Mr. Harris may just be a victim of circumstance," April explained. "A builder always hires contractors who in turn hire subcontractors. And I know he should have checked before he ordered the wrong septic tank and plumbing to be put in. It could have been an accident. In fact, I feel that it was."

"But the home buyers are still having to make payments on something they thought was correct when they made their purchase. That isn't fair. You're setting a precedent. Now they have to check into everything, right down to cabinet knobs." Sam leaned back and closed his eyes.

"No, the subcontractors should have to make the repairs, not the contractor, the builder or the home-owners." April turned to gaze at Sam and grinned. They looked like a matched pair. Which brought to mind her own personal problem. Jace.

"What's the heavy sigh for?" Sam asked lethargically, stretching his frame even more, so that the heels of his shoes could rest on the edge of her desk.

"How long have you been working for me?" April evaded Sam's question, needing time to gather her thoughts and put them into words.

"Four years," Sam answered promptly. "And if you're thinking about giving me a substantial raise, I'm all for it."

"How much longer do you have in law school?" she asked, evading that issue, also.

"Another semester. Then, Ms Flynn, I take my bar exam and become a certified attorney, along with being a certified nut. Thanks to you."

"Don't thank me. I'm not burning the midnight oil after working a full-time job all day. I'm through with that, thank goodness." She tried to pass his gratitude off with a brush of her hand in the air, but since both their eyes were closed, neither of them saw it.

"Oh? What *do* you call the work you do in the evening with the great movie star, what's his name? Oh, yes, Jace Sullivan." His voice was tinged with humor, and April smiled.

"Don't get fresh," she admonished sleepily. She ignored the fact that soon she had to get up from her comfortable position and drive home.

"Sorry," Sam said, his voice light with teasing. "Although I've had the pleasure of knowing you a year longer than he has, I'm afraid I don't know you half as well."

"Don't hand me that. I'm not your type and we both know it." She stifled a yawn.

"And that's my problem," Sam answered. "But what's yours? Something's been bothering you for the past few days. You've been preoccupied and moody. And don't tell me it's a case. I know better."

April opened both eyes and stared at the ceiling. Her mouth began to form words of explanation, but they didn't echo into the room. She frowned.

"Come on, I'm your best friend. You can tell me," Sam coaxed, a smile tilting his lips.

"Okay. It's Jace."

"What about him?" Sam's voice sounded his surprise at her answer. As far as he knew, they had found Eden.

"I want to marry him, but he hates marriage."

"Whew, you don't fool around with costume jewelry. You go right to the main, fourteen-karat-gold problem."

"So you think it's impossible, too." She closed her eyes again and took a deep gulp.

"No, I just think you could have tackled something else and had better results. Like turning a wild tiger into a domesticated kitten." His answer was dry, but his voice became thoughtful. "On the other hand, I don't think the problem's impossible to solve."

Her brows rose, her eyes still closed. "You don't?" Her voice showed she certainly hadn't found the answer to the problem and seriously doubted there was one.

"No. What you need to do is make sure you start acting more like a wife, instead of a live-in lover. If you want him to take you for a wife, you've got to be one. How the hell else is he going to know what he's missing if you don't give him a taste of it?"

"What does a wife do?"

"Oh, I don't know. I'd guess things like laundry before he needs it. Cooking his favorite dishes. Entertaining his friends. Picking out his clothing. You know, domestic things."

"I thought I hired a secretary and housekeeper for those things." April's voice was acerbic.

"Then you've just made *them* indispensable, not you," was Sam's lazy rejoinder.

"Oh, geez," she moaned, sitting up. His words hit home more than he realized. He was right. She had been so busy playing attorney and equal to the Great Jace Sullivan she hadn't even scratched the surface of playing "wife." At the rate she was going, she was damn lucky he was still interested in her and not tired of always having to make concessions to her schedule.

A small voice in the back of her mind told her she often had to do the same thing with his upside-down hours, but guilt, that powerful mind drug, wiped the notion out.

Sam opened his eyes and watched the myriad expressions cross her face. For an attorney, she was easy to read. Except for now. "What's going on in that beautiful head of yours?"

"I think you're right, Sam. In fact, I know you're right. I'm going to have to show him what he's missing by not marrying me. But I'm going to have to be so cagey that he never realizes that marriage is what I want."

" 'Man has his will—but woman has her way,' " Sam quoted in a deep baritone, pulling a slow reluctant smile from April.

"Exactly. If I can't get Jace to see the advantages of marrying me by the time we go on vacation, then I'm calling our relationship off. I'm twenty-nine. I'm not getting any younger and I want children, a home, a family, all the things that reek of middle-class values. But more than anything, I want Jace Sullivan." Her voice sounded wistful, longing.

"That's a new wrinkle in the April Flynn I know. You're usually so self-contained that I never knew you had a soft, motherly side to you." Sam's voice held a teasing note, for he sensed April had always had this side to her.

Over the years it had become more and more evident that her career was no longer the challenge it used to be. Nor was it as exciting. From Sam's observation, April's happiest moments were with Jace. And if the look that was usually plastered on Jace's face when he was with April was anything to go by, then Jace felt exactly the same way.

They were a lovely pair of fools.

"You love him very much." Sam's words drifted across the room.

"Yes." Her voice held a wealth of meaning. "Too much to continue this way." She ran a hand through her dark hair and it fell back into place as neatly as before. "It's getting harder and harder to live with this guilt I seem to have acquired. I also need more from him, Sam. I need his total commitment and the security of knowing we're a team, a pair. Together." She leaned back once more, wiggling deeper into the soft leather seat. "I know he was burned badly by his relationship with his mother and then again by his first marriage, but the way we're living now isn't the answer for me any more. I just don't know if my answer is right for him."

"Have you discussed this with him lately?" Sam asked, noting her blue expression.

"The last time was about a year ago. I brought up the subject and he very gently closed it. By the time I realized he hadn't really answered me, a week had passed and I was too embarrassed to ask him again."

"How could he get you so off track on such an important subject?" Sam queried, then raised his hand. "Never mind. I have a vivid imagination."

April grinned. "And your imagination would be right."

"In that case, both of you could have forgotten what the question was. Don't you think you should ask again? He may have changed his mind."

"He won't change his mind unless I start behaving more like a wife. Do you think they have schools I could attend to teach me to become a housewife?" she asked.

"No, I thought it was something women were born with. Maybe you're supposed to learn it at your mother's knee. Then again, that means that your mother would have to have learned it somewhere," he answered lazily, and they both chuckled at their silliness.

But still—a school would have helped. . . .

"Flynn?" Jace's voice drifted in from the outer reception area. "Where are you?"

"Right here," she called. Her energy was back. Her eyes still appeared tired and her voice wasn't as hearty as it could have been, but she'd definitely perked up.

Jace stood in the doorway, his eyes drinking her in. She looked weary. She looked bruised. She looked vulnerable. But she still looked so damn good he wanted to lay her down on the couch and make love to her right there. Common sense and Sam's shadow moving toward the bar gave him second thoughts. Instead he consoled himself with her kiss, bending over her chair and inhaling the scent of her first. At the same time he held out his hand for one of Sam's special margaritas. "Mmm, thanks, Sam."

April smiled, her expression teasing. "That's the first time Sam's been thanked for my kiss. I didn't know he had so much to do with it."

Sam's hands went in the air, palms up. "Don't hit me—I'm just an innocent bystander. Besides, she's my type, but she's not my type."

Jace smiled. It had taken a long time for him to overcome his jealousy of Sam. Sam and April were close, discussing not only office problems but personal ones, as well. But three years and not one out-of-line situation solved that. Sam was Flynn's best friend. Period.

Leaning down so only April's ears could hear his words, Jace whispered, "I was thanking him for the drink, Flynn, not the kiss. The kiss doesn't need thanks. It needs to be followed by another kiss. And another and another."

"I see," she murmured. "Did you film the love scene with that sexpot today?" she asked teasingly, as if that were the answer to his amorous advances.

"No, I didn't. I watched you in court today, then had lunch with my agent." He pulled her from her own seat and walked her to the couch, making sure she was curled up next to him as he placed an arm around her shoulder and pulled her toward him. She placed her head against his shoulder and gave a soft sigh. "Listening to you was enough to stir my blood."

"I hope the jury thought so."

Sam slipped out the door quietly, closing it behind him. They met at least three times a week this way. No one could call or get through to either of them; Sam saw to that. It was probably the only time they had completely alone when they weren't at home. Jace was too big a star to travel much farther than his own front door without being recognized, and April's clients were often the kind who called late at night. Family-court cases were her speciality.

Jace sipped his drink in companionable silence. Neither needed to create conversation. The quiet enfolded them in intimacy, creating an even stronger bond between them. They had each other; that was all that mattered.

April nuzzled into Jace's broad shoulder, loving the texture and scent of him.

He chuckled. "You remind me of a puppy the way you do that."

"And you remind me of a big hound. Your shoulders are twice as wide as they're supposed to be, and your height is indecent. Five-foot-five women are not supposed to date six-foot-three men. It's in the law books."

"You don't date me. You share my life and my bed.

You seem to match me very well when we're lying down," he teased. "Besides, when you're wearing those spikes you call 'heels,' you're almost as tall as I am." One hand spanned the front of her waist, his thumb and forefinger on each side of a rib. It slowly drifted up to just below her breast, sliding on the sensuous material of her dress.

"So. I'm good enough to share your bed, but I'm not good enough to date. Is that it?" Her voice was light, but somehow his words stung.

"Oh, Flynn, are you good enough!" His murmur echoed in her ear, turning her body to a warm, honeyed liquid with the intimation. "And to prove it to you, I'll take you anywhere you want to go. Tonight. Just name it and we're on our way."

April tilted her head, her bright blue eyes twinkling. She couldn't resist running a hand through his dark hair to rest in a teasing caress on his broad nape. "How about home? You can lie on the couch and read the paper while I put a big steak on the grill, toss a salad and microwave a potato. For dessert we'll invite Sara Lee." Her brow furrowed slightly. Was that the gourmet fare of a typical housewife? Somehow she doubted it. From the look on Jace's face he wasn't too thrilled with that idea, either.

"I thought we'd go somewhere romantic to eat. Maybe that little French restaurant you like so much—the one on the edge of town toward Malibu? Then I'll take you for a drive along the beach while I steal kisses from you. After that we could go home, light candles and make sweet, delicious love in front of the fire." His firm lips caressed her temple, working their way down the side of her neck to rest just above the cleavage of her breasts. Again the scent of her perfume drifted to him, reminding him of other parts of her body that were just as deliciously scented. She always put a splash behind her knees. . . . The thought of making love to her was enough to light his insides with a thousand glowing candles. His arms tightened around her.

"A fire? In September?" She sounded slightly breathless, which she was. His touch had the ability to raise her temperature on the hottest of days . . . or nights.

"We can always turn on the air conditioning," was his muffled answer. His tongue tasted the sweet saltiness of her cleavage. He breathed deeply again, the scent of her perfume making him even more aware of her. His cheek felt the softness of her skin.

Raising his head, his tongue dipped into the hollow of her ear, teasing her with a whispering warm breath and reminding her of other past actions that stirred a heat in her stomach. Memories of making love quickly brought those same needs to the surface.

Jace's lips skimmed her skin, sending shivers down his back as he realized just how addicted to her he had become. Now he knew his decision for them to marry was right. April Flynn was the only woman he wanted to hold in his arms. His hands splayed across her back, feeling the tension and texture of her. And he had made his decision just in time. She had behaved as a wife all through their relationship, and he had wanted it no other way. Now was the time to woo her into believing he was not only good-lover material, he was also the perfect husband. With her in his arms, that wasn't hard at all. . . .

April leaned back, loving the feel of his hands and mouth on her skin. She wanted him to touch her, to coax her. To love her. To love her enough to marry her.

That thought brought others tumbling forth, and her resolve to become the perfect wife once more was in the forefront of her mind.

"Wouldn't you rather spend a nice quiet evening at home, relaxing?" Her voice sounded like a hoarse whisper; her throat was closing with the intensity of the emotions he was arousing.

But a nagging fear was inching its way forward, too. Didn't he want to play husband to her wife? She'd never get him to realize how wonderful a wife she'd make if she didn't get rid of this sexpot image he had of her! She smiled. She certainly wasn't a sexpot, although Jace didn't seem to know it. His leading lady in the new comedy they were filming was a sexpot. Marilyn Monroe updated and recreated was Sandra Tanner's role. A twinge of jealousy ran through April, but she carefully hid it, squeezing his arms instead of giving him the sharp edge of her tongue for her own thoughts.

"I know what." Jace ran the tip of his finger just under the curve of her breast, leaving a trail of heat behind his touch. "I'll call the restaurant and have them deliver dinner to the house. That way neither one of us has to be, uh, distracted by other things."

"Fair enough." She sighed before the thoroughness of his kiss blocked out all other, more reasonable thoughts. His mouth was like a reverse hot-fudge sundae, all warm inside while the outside was cool from the icy margarita. His tongue darted circles in her mouth as he arched her closer to the leanness of his hard body.

"Mmm," she murmured, trying to tell him without words that she wanted him to continue his assault.

"Like that?" he muttered against her shoulder, more thick voiced than before.

"Oh, yes," she whispered back, her eyes closed as she felt every nerve he touched turn into a vibrant heat.

"There's more where that came from," he said, and his lips formed the perfect curvature to hers again, this time tightening, holding and possessing hers. His hands sought the rounded curves of her body, teasing, squeezing her into wanting to be even closer to him. One thumb flicked sweetly against her nipple, while another pressed low on her abdomen. He had only to stroke and she was ready for him. . . .

"You know what?" Jace whispered in her ear a few minutes later.

"What?" she whispered back.

"I hate Sam's margaritas."

"Sh. So do I."

Jace's dark brows rose. "Then why do you drink them?"

"Because it's the only drink he knows how to make and I hate to hurt his feelings."

Jace gave her a warm hug. "Oh, my Flynn. What an old softy you are," he said with a chuckle, shaking his head.

"I know, but so are you," was her retort. "After all, you've been drinking them for the past three years, too."

"Have we been together that long?"

April nodded. "That long."

He frowned, his thoughts darting. He had kept her with him for three years without a commitment. He was lucky she hadn't left before now, knowing how she used to feel about their arrangement. Three years was damn long enough to find out if they were suitable. Now he knew—they were perfect. It was time for action. "Well, my Flynn. It sounds as if we're due for a change. For the future, we need to look into something different."

Her heart beat quickly, fear surging through her body at his innocent words. "No change on the horizon that I can see, Mr. Sullivan. That is, unless you're talking drastic measures."

" 'Drastic.' Some might call them that, Flynn. But not me," he said, standing and pulling her up and into his arms. He grinned before he kissed the pert tip of her nose. "I call them 'Sullivanizing.' "

" 'Sullivanizing'?" Her voice broke over the word. Was this his way of tactfully telling her he was bored with their relationship? Was he hinting he had grown tired of her and felt he needed a change? Panic set her heart to beating quickly. She took a gulp and plunged in, ever ready to do battle for him by getting to know the enemy. "What does 'Sullivanizing' mean?"

"Later." He gave her a light slap on the rump. "Right now, Ms Attorney, I think we'd better head for home before I throw up Sam's drink." He glanced over at the offending glass sitting on the coffee table, a doubtful gleam in his eyes. "Three years, huh?" he murmured as if to himself. "My stomach must be in better shape than I thought."

April retrieved her purse and briefcase, and they walked slowly through the lobby and into the elevator together, both giving a silent wave to Sam, who sat at the front desk going over his notes for his class that night.

The evening was cool, with just a touch of wind stirring the air. After April made sure her car was locked, she stepped into Jace's sports car, leaning against the upholstery with a sigh. The air conditioning blew softly as he headed toward home, humming a slightly off-key rendition of an old Broadway tune.

Jace's house was snuggled in the canyons, a hilly area just east and slightly north of Los Angeles. He had had it custom-built several years ago, and it displayed his want of privacy along with a casual, carefree life-style. Constructed of adobe and wrought iron, it was all tans and pale, dull golds inside. A large courtyard was situated both in front and back, sealing off the world's gaze. The house clung to the side of the hill, fitting in with the peaceful but majestic scenery as if it were the missing piece of a jigsaw puzzle. Although Jace had designed it before he met her, April loved the place as much as he did. It gave them privacy, a view and a healing sense of self that communed with the nature surrounding them. While all the world at the base of the hills squabbled over the mundane, everyday things, Jace and April were wrapped in their own private world of peace.

Jace drove with care as he traversed the steep and narrow roads, shifting gears almost every minute as they continued to climb. All his attention was riveted on his second favorite pastime—driving the jet-black Alfa Romeo.

April leaned her head back, turning slightly so she could watch the concentration etched on his features. After three years she still loved everything about him.

She had met him at a party a client had given over four years ago. She was an established attorney with a small but fairly well-known practice that dealt with everyday family cases, not the usual royal and rich clients others sought. It was her very own practice and she loved it.

That night she had been rather impatient to leave. She'd felt out of place at the typical jet-setter party and just a little miffed that everyone who started a conversation wanted to know her astrological sign. It was either that or listen to the guests explain just how important everyone was, themselves included. Wasn't there anything else these people could discuss? She had silently decided to give herself another half hour and then depart, claiming work in the morning as her excuse.

But the minute Jace had walked in the door, all her attention had focused on him. His striking good looks were apparent to all, but it was his frown that caught her attention. He looked as bored to be there as she was, and she couldn't restrain the small, secret smile she had given him, telling that she understood and sympathized with his cool mood.

Something, some spark of kindred souls, had passed between them instantly. Eyes had riveted, her soft gray-blue blending with the sharp tobacco-brown of his. By the end of the evening he had managed to corner her and have a short conversation she couldn't even remember any more. They said words, but the real conversation was carried on with their eyes and hands and body movements. April had never been so completely in tune with a person before, and it not only surprised and frightened her, it was exhilarating! By the time the party was over, he had asked her to dinner the following night. She had accepted, wondering if she was crazy for doing so. An actor? What in the world would she have in common with an actor!

By the end of their first date she knew. Everything. His job, he had explained, wasn't much different from hers. He had to convince an audience, and she had to convince a judge and jury. What she saw on the screen was not him any more than she could be summed up as a person by what she said and did in court. They both had to prepare for what they did best, and it took hard work and dedication to do so. His logic was inescapable. She agreed with everything he said.

After they had dated for a little over two months, it was a shock to realize that when she thought they were heading toward the second step of loving, which was marriage, he had put a halt at the end of the first step. His explanation was given carefully, as if he were afraid of hurting her—though not enough afraid to change his mind on marriage. Yes, he loved her, but it didn't necessarily follow that he would marry. Marriage was for others, not him.

She never forgot the shock of his words. She had grown up an only child, secure in the love of her parents. All her life she had thought to have a career, yet a family, too. His aims stopped short of that. No wedding, no children. Just a nice, long, ongoing relationship. Once she found out about his past and the circumstances with his parents and then heard the story of his stormy first marriage, she realized he had seen nothing yet to change his opinions. She could understand his hesitancy and the conclusions he'd come to concerning the things she wanted most . . . marriage and children.

But understanding didn't make it easier; it made it harder. Everything she believed in went against the type of relationship he was proposing. He had asked her to live with him, taking for granted that she would be thrilled with the suggestion. Finally, in desperation, she'd broken away from Jace.

She could still remember the frustration in his voice. "I love you. I'm willing to commit myself to you and no one else. Doesn't that mean anything to you?"

"Not enough, Jace," she had quietly answered, her heart hurting as much as his did, but for different reasons. "I can't live with you. I can't."

"My God, you're twenty-six years old. Who's going to disapprove? Your parents?" His voice held contempt for that idea. "Aren't you a little old to ask permission? Aren't you a little old to seek someone's blessing for the life you have to live by yourself?"

"Perhaps. But I can't live with myself if I do what you ask."

It took four long months for April to look herself straight in the eye and examine what she was doing to herself. She had repeated silently over and over that she hadn't wanted to throw away her morals over an actor. The truth was that she was really holding out for marriage—something he apparently would never offer. Meanwhile she became thinner, less bubbly, quickly distracted. Every set of broad shoulders she saw on the street reminded her of Jace. Every dark head cocked in a certain way brought on a pounding in her blood. Every phone ring brought his voice to mind. Every night spent alone in her bed made her realize how empty her personal life was. Eventually she had to face facts. She could either continue this way, alone and lonely, or give in and contact him, placing her heart in his hands.

Luckily she didn't have to. Jace sent her a client who needed a trust fund set up for his son. Not one to miss an opportunity, April quickly sent Jace a note, thanking him. Then she sat back and clenched her hands for two weeks while she waited to see what he would do. If he didn't act by that time, she'd try calling.

Two weeks minus one day he phoned. He'd been out of town, filming in Mexico. How was everything going? Fine. Could he see her? Of course, she had replied calmly before hanging up and dancing on top of her desk. Sam had come in and made one of his special drinks, giving his support without words. He had seen the change in April since Jace had entered and left her life and knew that the only way she was going to be happy was to be with him. Under any conditions. If she could become a shadow of herself in just four months, he could imagine just what she'd look like at the end of the year.

One month later she was living with him, in his home and in his bed. Six months later she had signed a lease to rent her own house to another couple for the next two years. It was a total commitment for her. Her work was going well; her love life was even better than she'd dreamed possible. She was happy. But one thing hadn't changed: she still wanted marriage.

JACE TURNED INTO THE DRIVEWAY, gunning the engine to make the steep grade. "Home," he pronounced in a satisfied voice after pulling to a stop. He leaned back and looked at her, his brown eyes softening as he took in her tiredness.

"I could feel your eyes on me the whole trip." His voice was low and husky. "What were you thinking?"

"I was remembering when we met."

"And how high-handed I was in getting you into my very lonely bed?"

She smiled, her hand coming up to tease a brown sideburn. "Something like that," she hedged.

His dark eyes turned even darker. "And are you sorry I led you into a life of sin, Flynn?"

"I don't know." Her answer was honest. "I just know that I love you very much and I wasn't doing all that well without you."

"Neither was I," was his ardent admission before he took her into his arms and held her comfortingly close to his chest. She rested there, totally content. His hands moved on the small of her back, comforting, stroking. His lips grazed her temple before his cheek rested on the top of her head. She could hear the quickened beating of his heart and she loved it.

They sat quietly like that for a few minutes, watching the sunset out the front window, enclosed in each other's love and clasp. It was so perfect, so wonderful. But doubts concerning her new plans for marriage began to form again. Was she doing the right thing in forcing him into a role he filled in all but name only? Was it fair to him? She didn't know. All she knew was that she was still, in some dark portion of her mind, unhappy. His lack of legal commitment hurt, more than words could say. It was as if he didn't want to tell the world he loved her.

"I love you, Ms Flynn." He sighed contentedly into her ear.

"I love you, too, Mr. Sullivan," was her soft answer as she smiled and gave his chest a light kiss.

"Then let's go in the house, get naked and lie in a pile before the restaurant man comes."

She giggled, her hands tightening on his arms so she could snuggle closer. "Is this the same man who told me only yesterday he had over thirty scripts to read before the end of the month?"

"The same. But you know what they say about all work...." He leered, bringing another giggle to her lips.

A car's headlights beamed at them from behind.

Jace gave a heavy sigh. "Well, so much for naked. Here's the man with the food."

"Curses, foiled again," April quipped in her best

villain's voice. "That's okay, darling," she consoled him. "Soon we'll have all month to do nothing but commune with nature and each other." She crossed her fingers, hoping they would be communing together. She was wavering in the promise she had made to herself, but she resolved to stick by it. She had to take a stand sometime—it might as well be now.

"You don't know how much I need that time with you." His voice was husky with need as he gave a light squeeze before reluctantly pulling away and opening the door. "Meanwhile we have to eat, sleep and live in this convoluted world. Come on, lady mine. It's time to join the living."

The food was delicious, crepes and pâté and French pastry with their coffee. They ate and talked and sipped wine on the front patio, watching the sunset as they relaxed away the day. After dinner, he straightened up the kitchen while she did a quick load of laundry. The housekeeper had been ill the past week, and it looked as if she wouldn't be able to return for another two or three weeks.

Then, with soft music on the stereo, they both studied: she worked on a new case, while he read scripts. The quiet was peaceful, pervading her senses with a calmness she hadn't felt all day. Every once in a while she would glance up to find him looking at her, a question darkening his eyes. She'd smile reassuringly, and he'd answer with a grin all his own. Then they'd both begin reading again.

She closed her eyes in a silent plea for him to notice what a good wife she would be. Could marriage be as bad for him as their present living arrangement was for her? He seemed to thrive on this type of relationship, but it was eating her alive. If only he could see just how *right* they were for each other. . . .

"Come on, you. When you close your eyes, I know it's time for you to go to bed." Jace's voice was filled with a chuckle. His hand clasped hers, and he pulled her up and into the strength and security of his arms.

"But I'm not sleepy," she protested groggily, snuggling her head into his broad shoulder. She rested her arms on his trim waist, loving the feel of his muscles against her flesh. His hand molded to the small of her back, rubbing slowly and methodically. His lips touched the top of her head in a quiet, reassuring kiss.

He pulled away and grinned, obvious other activities on his mind. "Neither am I, but bed is still the prescription."

Slowly they walked down the wide hallway, checking the lock on the front door, then flicking out the lights as they passed.

By the time they reached the bedroom, April was in the same mood as Jace—ready for some slow, sweet loving.

Jace's loving.

2

THE FRENCH DOORS LEADING from the pool area to the darkened bedroom were open. The cool night breeze filtered through to stir and ruffle the loose-weave curtains. The air was scented with a mixture of overspilling jewel-colored flowers in large red clay pots that dotted the patio and the chlorine that kept the pool clean.

Shadows darkened the room, but enough diffuse light came from the patio security-lighting system to soften the hand-carved, yet simple Mexican-style furniture outlined against the stark-white bedroom walls. The wide, rough beams overhead looked as if they actually held up the ceiling. Everything was black and white—except the two of them.

They stood silently staring at each other, each anticipating the motions of love that were to come. Almost shaky hands, gentled by love, undressed her unhurriedly. Jace would bare a spot, then stop to feel the soft texture of her skin there. He would move on with reluctance, only to do the same thing again in a different place. April stood very still, etched against the light coming from the patio door, her blue eyes watching his as they'd discover a dark mole or a curve. A faint sigh or small smile would underline his pleasure.

"You like?" she asked softly.

"I love," was his husky-voiced answer. His lips caressed her briefly. Then he took off another article of clothing and watched her reactions as he stroked her to his way of thinking. Each touch, each kiss was a symbol of their caring for each other.

Unable to stand not touching him, too, she began to undo the buttons of his shirt. One by one she slipped them through the holes, exposing his lightly furred chest and the muscles of his ribs to her gentle, wandering touch. Her hands shook with longing; her stomach bunched with nerves that had been awakened by his nearness. He halted his movements, thrilling to the way her eyes turned from blue to gray as she became attuned to his body. Fingertips felt for his heartbeat before skimming over flat male nipples that grew erect at her touch. She trembled with the anticipation of feeling his skin next to hers. It was always like this when she was with him. Always.

Then, equaling the excitement he had shown, she unbuckled his belt and unzipped his zipper. She felt his breath hold, only letting out slowly as her hands passed from his waist to his hips, shedding the barriers of clothing. Soon they were both exposed to the night and each other, standing just scant inches away from meeting flesh to flesh.

They teased each other with the distance, seeing how long they could bear not being together, anticipating their union. Her response to him began deep inside her, tingling and aware, while his was visible...and made him even more endearingly vulnerable. They stared through the muted darkness at each other, their eyes sending messages their mouths couldn't say. Minutes passed, seeming like hours, as they reaffirmed silent words of love and promised so much more to come. Tension filled the air with the earthy, heady-scented perfume of love.

Jace was the first to move, to give in to the need to touch again, to reestablish their connection. His large hand trailed her arm, then rested lightly on her hip, giving a light squeeze. "I love you like this, all warm and golden, bathed in soft light that seems to glow from deep inside you, instead of outside."

She shook her head slowly in lieu of an answer. Her voice wouldn't work. She couldn't stop looking at him, staring into his eyes to read the message plainly written there. His brown eyes blazed with a quiet but desperate need for only her. Her hands trembled on his chest; her nails lightly bit the circle of his nipples, as if silently communicating through actions what she wanted him to do to her.

Finally, inevitably, his hands tightened on her hips and he brought her toward him and into the intimate contact of his body, of his need. His arms encased her to fit and mold to his leaner, firmer build. Skin touched skin from chest to thighs.

He tilted her chin up for easier access to her slightly parted mouth, kissing her as if he would never let her go. She melted toward him, her body becoming warm fluid as his tongue dueled in sweet slow motion with hers.

Silent messages once more passed between them as the anticipation of their lovemaking seemed to arc the air with electricity. Then he pulled back to gaze once more into her eyes. His tongue outlined her lips, teasing her with his nearness while holding back with a control she had always envied.

"Jace," she murmured. Her heart was beating a primitive drumbeat through her body. Her control was almost gone.

"I know, I know. Stop teasing." He chuckled huskily, only the tremor in his voice showing the amount of restraint he was exerting. "But I love to watch you, to take you on every step of the way, darling. I don't want to miss a thing."

Her eyes closed and once again he took her lips, his hands lowering to her hips to bring her into closer contact with his need. His mouth asserted pressure and she opened to him, craving the intimate touch of his tongue and lips. Her low, satisfying moan echoed inside his mouth to touch his very soul.

Her legs were turning to rubber; her heart pace speeded up with every move his muscles made. He felt it, and with a low, answering moan deep in his throat, he picked her up and carried her to the large bed, laying her across it. He leaned over her, his body braced on one arm while his other hand traced the soft and gentle curves of her. His hand moved constantly, as if to reassure himself she was really there, almost beneath him. Then slowly he retraced his steps, beginning to savor this kind of contact as much as the act of love itself. He outlined her neck, slowly easing his hand between her breasts, lightly touching her navel, before bringing it to rest on the soft mound of her.

Then with quiet deliberation his mouth followed

the same path. Her muscles turned to molten lead, then tensed to spring alive under his persistent touch. Blood sped through her body at such a fast rate her heart could barely keep pumping. His hands and mouth were everywhere, nowhere, then everywhere again.

She took his head in both her hands and led him back to her breast, twisting her shoulders so that his mouth would have easier access. Warm tongue and light gentle sucking brought her close to the edge as he slowly moved from one silken globe to the other. He lavished his attention on both so that neither would be slighted, and she moaned her response.

Her hands clenched his shoulders as he continued carrying her over the invisible threshold they had crossed many times before. His hand sought and played with her, tuning her for the final act. His fingers created a wonderful magic as she arched to meet their gentle thrust, wishing he would take her completely instead of using his creative hand as a substitute.

Breathing was becoming unnecessary. She felt as if she were floating on a cloud. Her voice rasped in her throat, as if she were parched for his loving. "Jace, yes, yes."

"I know, darling," was all he could say, for his own need was spiraling so quickly he had to lie quietly beside her for a moment. His breath echoed in her ear, and her heart beat in cadence to it. She held him close, the muscles of her body quivering from his touch. Her body arched to meet the thrust of his, trying to burrow into his skin so they could become one.

Still he held back.

Slowly he began again, his hands and mouth working her over as if she were the only sustenance he needed to live. She arched, her whole being crying out in need, and his answer was a throaty, triumphant chuckle that echoed through the room.

"Now!" she pleaded, and he finally obliged, almost drowning her in his lean, hard flesh as he covered her with his heated body. His mouth clamped on hers in a kiss as desperate as the cravings of their bodies.

They fitted so perfectly. Floating together, arms and bodies entwined, they touched souls, and both knew it at the same moment. Arms tightened, sighs lengthened and soon a healing completeness bound them to each other. The air was finally silent as they both began the slow descent back to earth.

Forehead to forehead, they each caught the other's breath and held it before expelling it, to be caught again. His lips moved silently over her brow, her temples, her closed eyes. They stopped when he touched her cheeks and found them wet with salty tears.

"April?" His voice was still shaky with the aftermath of their loving. He leaned the bulk of his weight on his arms, pulling his head back to stare down at her. "What is it? Tell me."

She shook her head, denying anything was wrong. She loved him so much but couldn't find the words to say what she needed from him.

He rolled his weight off her and turned on his side so he could better see her face. Taking her into the haven of his arms, his hand soothed her hair back from her forehead. Her mouth touched his chest and he gave a light squeeze, silently telling her how much he loved to hold her close.

"Tell me," he said, genuine concern now filling his voice. "Let me help. Did I hurt you?" He pushed her bangs aside, again stroking her forehead as he did so.

"No," she muttered, trying to keep the tears at bay. "It was so beautiful."

"But that's not why you're crying." It was a statement, not a question.

"Yes, it is," she lied, pulling him back to her and resting her cheek on his chest.

They lay in silence in the quiet room, listening to their heartbeats revert slowly to normal. The French doors were still open and the night chill was finally penetrating the room. Jace reached down and pulled the sheet over both of them, then took her in his arms once more. He leaned his chin against the top of her head and, with a frown marring his brow, closed his eyes. He could tell by April's even breathing that she was already asleep. His arm brought her closer. Silently he wished she could crawl inside his skin and stay there with him. Always. He lightly felt her cheeks. The tears had dried; her skin was smooth.

What went wrong? He had made love to her with all his heart, trying to show her without words just how deep his love was and how much she meant to him. Where had he gone wrong? Were the tears her way of telling him she didn't love him as strongly as he loved her? A sharp pain pierced his chest at that thought. Could she be bored by his lovemaking motions, having known them for the past three years?

Perhaps she was just playing a role for his benefit because she didn't know how to get out of this relationship? No. That wasn't it. He knew an honest response, and hers was just that. He also knew April Flynn, and she was no pretender. She was direct and caring. She was no actress who tried to soothe him when there were hard times; why would she when they made love? She was one of the few people he knew who was like that. It was the first thing that drew him to her.

He remembered the first night they'd met. It was at a party given to gain his attention for a movie script his agent wanted him to consider. He had gone under duress, swayed by his agent's earnestness about the property. Walking into a room filled with strangers was one of the things he most disliked about the movie business. He didn't know a soul at the party except the host, but everyone knew him through his movies and expected him to greet them like old friends.

Then he felt a pair of eyes on him from across the room. They never seemed to waver from his face. Finally, irritated by the direct stare, he glanced up and returned her look. Brilliant blue eyes laughed back at him. It was as if she were pitying him. Pity! No one had the right to pity him! He had been furious at the time, but had carefully hidden his anger behind a professional, benign smile—the kind he gave to the heroines in his films. It had worked. Her pity had changed to a kind of shared sympathy in the space of that glance, and she was suddenly, silently, conspiring with him against all the other guests. He had promised himself then and there that he would meet her, just for the pure fun of it.

He did. Only she caught him in her web, instead of the other way around.

His being an actor had never entered into their relationship any more than his being a plumber or doctor would have. That fact fascinated him. She was neither awed nor put off by his occupation. For the first time in his adult life that he could remember, he was sought after for himself. She shared herself with him and automatically expected him to do the same with her. She was not overwhelmed by his name dropping or his status in the movie world. To her he was just a man she had met and enjoyed. Amazing. But even more amazing was the fact that that was what he wanted, too. He'd had all the adoration that went with his business, and it had always left him wanting something else. Now he knew what it was. It was strange to think that at his age he still wanted to be accepted for who he was and not what he was.

They had left the party and he had taken her for a drive. Somewhere along the way, they had stopped the car and talked quietly, the windows rolled down and the evening breeze filtering through to ruffle her hair softly. Her bright blue eyes twinkled with a sense of humor and sympathetic understanding of the words he *wasn't* saying. Again, it was amazing to him.

He had kissed her then. Whether it was by accident or by design—he wasn't sure—he had fumbled. Perhaps in the back of his mind he had thought to test her to see if she compared the sophisticated lover of the screen with his bumbling efforts in real life. But she had passed with flying colors, chuckling and then holding him close, as if he had been an adorable, precocious child. But already his blood was thumping like a pumpjack giving oil.

He had never wanted anyone as badly as he had wanted her that night, and almost had to push her away to keep from fulfilling his own promise to tread carefully. She was different from anyone he had ever been with, and he could not stand the thought of losing her before he got to know what he was losing.

By their third date he was salivating at the very thought of touching her again. He had never done that before! He had to face the fact that he had never been so affected by any woman up to that point. He didn't know what to think.

By their fourth date he was finally where he wanted to be, in her arms and in her bed, and being with her was better than he had ever believed it could be. By the end of two months he knew he had to have her live with him. From the beginning he had wanted her body next to his in a big, soft, comfortable bed, but now he found that he wanted her with him when he read, ate, watched tv. Or just to talk to. He had never ever felt that way about any woman before. When he asked her to live with him, he'd been confident of her answer, and was stunned when she turned down his offer.

After the shock wore off he was angry. Who the hell did she think she was? There were plenty of other women out there who would *die* to get into his bed and life! Didn't she know who he was? Then came depression. What had he done wrong? Hadn't he wooed her, holding himself back for longer than he had ever done for any woman? Hadn't he been ardent, tender, loving? Giving more of himself, his private self, to her than he had ever given to *any* woman? Then his disappointment turned to anger again.

Finally, when a deal came through for him to do a few cameo shots for a new movie being filmed in Mexico, he jumped at the chance. Leaving the city was the only way he could stop himself from driving past her house late at night and playing the role of a Peeping Tom. Only he hadn't been acting. He had to get her out of his system.

Leaving didn't work, either. For weeks he tried to figure out a way to get her back in his arms and by his side, where she belonged. When a phone call came from Joel, one of his good friends, asking that he read another script, he made Joel promise that in turn he would set up some legal deal and put it through Ms April Flynn, attorney. And part of the deal was that Jace had to be mentioned as having referred Joel to her.

Then he sat back, and with teeth bared and nails sharpened on everyone else's hide, he waited. He had told everybody he would still be out of town for a while. In reality, he spent two weeks shut up in his home as if it were a jail. Two of the most lonely, awful weeks of his life. At the end of the first week he received a letter from her. He knew because it was on her office stationery. Propping it on top of the mantel, he stared at it for hours at a time.

It took three days before he could gather up the nerve to open it. He could laugh now, but who would have thought that the Great Jace Sullivan, the man who could defy spies, villains, sex goddesses and nature, didn't have the courage to read one damn letter!

Once again the door was open and their relationship had a chance. He called her right away, making a date she couldn't refuse, one on neutral ground at a restaurant she loved. That was a crazy period. It took five days for them to get back together. He couldn't believe his good fortune when she finally admitted that she loved him and would live with him. He still remembered the look on her face, and it verified everything that she'd said. He thought the days were over of experiencing such a terrible wanting that ate away deep in the gut. But he was wrong.

Now, three years later, he still wasn't satisfied. Now he wanted her to share his name, to commit herself to him completely. That was what she had wanted in the beginning, too. Only somehow, over the years their relationship had grown, and she seemed to have given up the thought of marriage and now felt as he had once. If tonight was anything to go by, it would be an uphill climb to convince her she needed to be married after all these years of living with him.

It was a shame he couldn't enjoy the joke, since he had to laugh at himself. It had taken him almost a year to persuade April she should live with him without marriage. Now that he had done such a fine job, he had to try to change her mind about their arrangement and hope that she would marry him.

He gave a heavy sigh and tightened his hold on her waist. He'd have to be the world's best salesman, as well as the world's best lover, so she wouldn't want to leave him. He frowned again. Somehow the idea didn't appeal to him . . . it sounded too much like acting, when the roller-coaster emotions he was dealing with were all too real.

THEY WOUND DOWN THE CANYON DRIVE, April sipping her coffee as Jace drove expertly. Since he had picked her up from work last night, she had to have a ride back to her car. She had forgotten how early he had to be on the set. How he did it every day he worked was beyond her. Five in the morning seemed like midnight. She yawned.

Jace grinned. "It's the penalty you pay for a night of insatiable loving."

"It's the price I pay for allowing you to drive me home," she retorted.

"Aw, you're more awake than I thought. Your mind's already going a mile a minute."

"So is your car," she answered, watching him competently maneuver a narrow turn. He immediately slowed down.

They drove for a few more minutes in silence. Then Jace broke it, clearing his throat first before giving her a quick, innocent look. "Flynn?"

"Mmm?"

"Have you ever thought about children?"

He didn't see the wary look she gave him. He was too busy watching the next curve and shifting gears in tune with the powerful engine. "In what way?" she asked.

"Oh, I don't know." He shrugged his broad shoulders and settled better into the bucket seat. "Any way."

"Occasionally," she hedged, knowing that the thought had occurred to her far more than she cared to admit. A child like Jace, with blue eyes and curly dark hair, deep dimples. . . .

"When?"

"When I see one."

"How often is that?"

"I don't know. In a restaurant, shopping, in the park when I eat my lunch outside."

"What do you think of them? In general, I mean."

He was persistent; she'd give him that. But there was no way she was going to agree to have a child out of wedlock! If he wanted a child he could just find someone else to have one for him! That thought made her clench her hands. Just let him try! "I think children are nice," she answered sweetly, grabbing for the door as he made another sharp turn.

"Is that all?"

"What do you expect me to say, Jace?" Now it was his turn to answer a few questions! What was behind all this? Hadn't he told her he didn't *want* children? Another thought struck her. Did he think she was pregnant? She had gained a few pounds lately, but she had thought it was flattering to her. She had always been so underweight. Did he not like those pounds?

"I don't know. I just wondered." He stole a quick glance at her before bringing his attention back to the road.

"What do you think about children?"

"They're, uh, very nice."

She sat up and smiled brightly, hiding her anger at his bringing up a topic she had thought of privately and too often. "Well, that's one subject we agree upon."

He darted a glance at her. "What do you mean?" Now he was the wary one.

"I mean that we both agree that children are 'nice,'" she said cheerfully. Mentally she was thinking of ways she could someday scare the heck out of him as he was doing to her with this conversation on this narrow road.

Not another word was said during the rest of the drive to her office. But when Jace pulled up in front of the office door, he slammed the car into park and reached for her. His kiss was harsh, quick and desperate, and somehow made him very vulnerable. His touch was almost hurting. The kiss was also unexpected.

"Take care, Flynn," he said huskily as he pulled away. Then he reached out, outlining her slightly parted lips with his finger. His dark-brown eyes burrowed into hers. He was giving her a message, but she couldn't interpret it. It was written in a code only he could understand.

She gave him a reassuring smile. "You, too, Jace," she murmured before climbing out and walking toward the door without a backward glance.

SAM WALKED IN THE DOOR around eight-thirty, to find all the lights on and the aroma of freshly brewed coffee in the air. Hands on lean hips, he stood and looked at his desk, piled high with files he knew hadn't been there the night before. He walked through the outer reception area and opened the door to April's office.

She was sitting in her desk chair, her hands wrapped around a mug of coffee. Her stare out the window resembled a trance more than someone deep in thought.

"My, my. The attorney is early this morning. It's a good thing I was on time today."

"Hello, Sam." April continued to look out the window at the building across the street. It was a deep-purple, four-story stucco structure that sold the most wonderfully indecent lingerie for women. Perhaps that was what she needed. No, scratch that thought. Jace would only take lingerie off the way he'd taken her clothing off last night. She'd wait and buy sexy underthings at a time when he wasn't interested in her anymore. A pain jabbed at her from deep in her breast.

Sam glanced around. "Want a refill on that coffee?"

She held out the empty mug. "Thanks," she said, still staring out the window.

Only when the mug was placed back in her hands did she slowly swivel her chair around and look at him.

"My God, what happened to you!" Sam exclaimed, his gaze narrowing to take in her swollen eyes and blotchy skin. "You look like someone used your face as a punching bag!"

"I've been crying."

"Why?" Sam's eyes turned a chilly brown. "Did Jace

do something to you?" he growled. His voice held so clear a threat toward the other man that April had to give an attempt at a smile. Sam was protective of all women, and more so with her.

"Nothing I didn't want." She stood, and with both hands on her waist, she stretched. She had been sitting in almost the same position for over an hour. Her muscles were cramped.

"In that case, how's the campaign going?" Sam might not believe her, but he wasn't about to open that can of worms...yet.

"Not too well, Sam." Her voice held a wistfulness he hadn't heard since April and Jace had been together.

"What happened? Tell Uncle Sam," he quipped, bringing another smile to her lips.

"Nothing much. I was going to act domesticated and cook dinner last night, but he sent out for French food. Then, since the housekeeper's been ill, I was going to be domesticated and do the wash. Only Jace wound up with pink underwear. Then I was going to play the housewife and fall asleep before he came to bed, but that didn't work, either."

Sam barely hid his smile. April had enough to contend with besides his laughter. It dawned on him that she really needed lessons from someone on how to be a wife. She had never had the chance since her career had taken up most of her time. But her education was definitely lacking. "What happened to the underwear?"

"I left it soaking in bleach. If the pink isn't out by tonight, then I'll buy him new underwear."

"Just bleach, or bleach and water?"

She looked up, her eyes wide. "Just bleach. Why, is that wrong?"

"Not if it's only for a few minutes, April. But I have a feeling that by the time you get home that underwear will look holey . . . and I don't mean religious."

"Damn!" she muttered under her breath. "Why didn't my mother bother to teach me these things! Instead she always did them for me, and then my maid took over when I left home and opened up my own law practice." Her misery was apparent as she reviewed what she had done.

Sam couldn't help teasing; it was almost irresistible. "And I thought all women were born knowing how to wash clothes and cook. Something to do with the genes."

"Not this lady. I've only done my own laundry since last week, when Jace's housekeeper got sick and went to the hospital. Apparently some of his knit shirts aren't supposed to be laundered but sent out. I didn't know. This is all new to me."

"And how does the Great Jace take all this?" Sam prodded gently. He could tell by the look in her eyes that he hadn't prodded gently enough.

She winced at the thought. "My bungled attempts don't seem to bother him at all. He just grins." She sighed heavily. "Jace acts the perfect lover, spurning all my attempts to domesticate him." She looked at Sam, her blue eyes clouding to a dusty gray. "I don't think my plans for leading Jace toward marriage are going to work, Sam, and I'm scared to death of losing him."

"I doubt that will happen," he said dryly, remembering the smoldering looks Jace had given her just last evening. That wasn't the look of a man who would let go of his woman easily. Somehow he thought of Jace as a terrier with a bone when it came to April Flynn. He'd never give her up gracefully. He'd never give her up, period. All the signs were there, only April couldn't see them.

"I don't," she practically wailed. "Not only that but, but, he asked what I thought of children!"

"What's wrong with that?" Sam's brows rose. "It sounds hopeful to me."

"Just six months ago he was telling a friend of his how silly he thought marriage was, and now he talks about children! He isn't changing his mind about marriage! He's just decided he wants a family without the benefit of commitment!" Suddenly her hurt was gone, replaced by anger. How dared he put her in such a position! Why, if he loved her half as much as he pretended. . . .

"Oh, my heavens!" she said softly, then stared up at Sam again. "You don't think he's trying to break off our relationship, do you, Sam?" Without waiting for an answer, she continued. "Then there was the kiss this morning. It was almost as if he were testing himself to see what his reaction would be. Or maybe it was a goodbye kiss and he was really hurrying to get to the set so he could be with that damn actress!"

She stood up in agitation, then sat back down hard in her chair. "That's it. He really wants to break it off, but he feels guilty about putting me in this position of his mistress in the first place. He's just not sure how to go about it." Her voice ended in a dead whisper; her blue eyes had become larger, showing her dismay with every word uttered.

"All that circumstantial evidence comes from a logical, fact-seeking attorney?" Sam's voice broke into her reverie. "I think I just heard the plot for the week on a soap opera, not the life and love of April Flynn!"

Her eyes gleamed hopefully, willing to grasp at any straw. She sat up straighter. "Do you think I'm just imagining it all?"

"Yes, I think so," he said in a tone laced with false sternness. "And I'm surprised at you. You usually are so demanding in your search for evidence. The man in this office last night had no thoughts of breaking off a relationship. He loves you, April. I'm sure of it."

Her mouth curled into a smile as she remembered their night together. He had wooed her into that bed as gently as any man possibly could. His actions were definitely not those of a man bored with his lover. She frowned. Or were they?

"Sam, if I ask you a personal question, will you answer me truthfully?" Her voice was hesitant, thoughtful.

"Ask me and then I'll tell you. But I warn you, if it ruins my image as a hardworking, intelligent male on his way into his own practice, I'll plead the Fifth Amendment."

"How do you act when you're bored with a relationship?"

"Bored," was his prompt reply.

"I'm serious! Do you try to resurrect that feeling you had for her in the beginning?"

"No. I usually feel guilty and try to cut the relationship off quickly so I won't be reminded of my guilt."

"Then you don't try to recapture that glow of first love?"

"I never went through 'the glow' of first love with any of the women I dated except my first-grade teacher. And I'm not sure about that." He grinned unrepentingly. "I only know good, honest lust when I see it."

"You're no help."

"Yes, I am," he protested. "I'm telling you that no man tries to 'resurrect' love when he doesn't feel it unless he has nowhere else to go. In that case, he looks around and sees about finding a replacement, not recapturing something he doesn't want."

"Oh." She finally understood. "But could you make love to a woman you were tired of?"

"Sure, if she put a bag over her head and pretended to be Mae West," was his answer. She looked up at him, trying to find a hint of mischief lurking in his eyes. He wasn't teasing.

"So all I have to do is watch and see if Jace puts a bag over my head or tries to replace me with another woman in his life."

"Believe me, April, that's not what he would do. He'd get rid of you first. No man wants two complications in his life at the same time. That spells trouble with a capital *T*. Besides, I think you're trying to take the wrong road to get to Lovers' Lane."

"I'm already at Lovers' Lane. I want Marital Bliss Street."

"Your directions are still wrong." He shook his head as if talking to a recalcitrant child. "You're trying to figure out Jace's next move when you should be plotting your own. Jace loves you. All you have to do is play a better game of chess, and his pawns will drop in your lap like raindrops."

"Except that I want the king," she retorted dryly.

"You have to get rid of the externals before you can find the Big One." At her startled look, he grinned sheepishly. "No pun intended."

The phone rang and the work day began. April had to be in court by ten to defend her case, and Sam and she were both busy trying to ease other clients into an already-filled calendar.

Somewhere between the clients and court duties, April still had to figure out what to do about her relationship with Jace. She had known him for more than three years, and yet she felt as if she didn't know him at all. She had to scout out the enemy better, if she was to win the big prize. Everything she cared about depended on her next step toward her goal. Questions churned around in her brain, but she couldn't come up with the answers.

She gave a heavy sigh every five minutes. Sam was right. Thinking about it wasn't enough. She had to take action.

Should she continue to be devious, or should she just come out and propose to him, leaving games to others? No, he'd never accept the proposal plan—after all, he'd turned that thought down three years ago and made her play by his rules. She'd have to find a way to make her rules more attractive, more fun, more....

She leaned back and closed her eyes.

It was going to be another hectic day.

3

TUESDAY TURNED OUT TO BE a red-letter day after all. All her talent, hard work and concentration paid off. April won her case and was out of court early.

"Congratulations!" Sam said, grinning from ear to ear over her ability in clearing the builder. He didn't have to agree with the verdict to be happy for her.

"Thank you, sir. I just had a very intelligent jury and a marvelous crew to hold down the fort while I did my homework."

"And a smart mind that saw the logic the jury would buy," Sam added dryly, perching himself on the seat of the chair in front of her desk.

"Well, I won't deny that," she said with a laugh. "Think you can close the office this evening?"

"I can't, but I can show one of the girls how to close and pick up the key from her later." His grin told her he had plans for that "later." "Why?"

"I'm starting on the major campaign tonight. I've got to be on my way if I'm going to be ready by the time Jace comes home."

"Well, good luck. If your case against Jace is as air-tight as your case was this morning in court, you won't have any trouble."

"Thanks, but if you've got any weight at all with

the gods that be, call upon them in my name, will you? I'm going to need all the help I can get on this one," she said as she grabbed her purse and briefcase and headed toward the door, her step jaunty. "I'll see you in the morning, Mr. Lewis."

She left the office, assured that Sam and the secretary, Joanne, had everything under control. He had the whole office running efficiently, including the two part-time girls, who had a backlog of work to file and type, so there was no need to worry.

April ticked off the mental list of items she needed to do before heading for home. One: she had to find a supermarket whose employees knew more about cooking than she did. Two: she had to buy a good bottle of wine. Three: she had to vacuum the living room and sweep the kitchen before Jace came home.

With the deep sigh of one who was climbing mountains never scaled before, she pulled into a small but chic market, hoping the clerks knew enough about cooking that they could help her prepare a gourmet meal with her limited amount of knowledge. In the future she would take a cooking course, but right now she had to take action. . . .

An hour later, laden with two bags of groceries, April knew she had chosen the right store. Tonight she was going to serve *Fricassée de Saint-Jacques à l'anis*, with a side dish of buttered spinach noodles. The vegetable would be canned asparagus . . . expensive, but it could hardly be messed up.

The clerk's help and step-by-step instructions for the recipe of sea scallops in a rich cream sauce were invaluable, to say nothing of the frilly, white apron that made her look domesticated *and* sexy, if that could be accomplished with one small piece of material. She grinned as she remembered the older salesclerk's stern warning that had been accompanied by a bawdy wink. "And remember, always wear high heels. If you wear nothing but the apron, wear high heels. Men love it!"

Next, on to number two. Within twenty minutes she was pulling out of the liquor store with what the owner assured her was the perfect wine for before dinner, for her entrée and for after dinner. Jace would be nothing if not pliant! She just hoped he wouldn't be too drunk to notice her efforts.

Now home to ready for number three. It wasn't as glamorous as one and two, but it was necessary nonetheless. She didn't want him to eat this damn meal and then ravish her body on the carpet in front of the fireplace only to become distracted by the dirt! She mentally patted herself on the back. She was thinking ahead now, capturing every pawn that lay in her way.

Why did winning Jace seem more of a challenge than the court case she had just finished? She didn't know, but remembered something her mother used to say: "It's not the pieces of the puzzle that fit that are important, April, dear. It's the pieces that aren't fitting properly that give you the most trouble." It was true. Her business life was orderly. It was her personal life that she wanted to change, and therefore it became her biggest problem.

By the time Jace was due home she had cleaned, begun the cooking, iced down the martinis and wines and placed her small scrap of an apron over her black dress and around her tiny waist. She tottered over to the mirror in her highest of high, black-patent heels to check her appearance. Her dark-brown hair framed her face like a cloche. Her makeup was more dramatic than usual, but not overdone. Her figure, trim—this was better than saying thin. She squinted, seeing if she could see those extra pounds she had gained. Nope. The angular lines were still there. She gave another sigh. Why couldn't she look like a movie star?

"April Flynn. You're cute and sexy, but you'll never be a gorgeous sex symbol," was the mirror's telepathic reply, and because she couldn't think of a retort, she stuck out her tongue at her reflection.

She waited until Jace was almost an hour late before calling the studio. Mr. Sullivan was in a meeting with the writers. He didn't say when he'd be through. They were not to be disturbed. He would be told of her call when he left the meeting. . .thank you for calling.

She called an hour later and it was the same answer, only this time a different girl.

By nine that night she was in the kitchen tasting her own wares. She threw the fork down. Wouldn't you know it was the best dinner she had ever cooked and no one was here to appreciate it! How could he do this to her! It didn't matter that he hardly ever remained late at work; that was incidental to her beautiful dinner. Highly appropriate names for Jace Sullivan flitted through her head, but she was too miserable to dwell on them long. Self-pity was easier and took less thought and effort.

By ten she had changed into her robe and was sipping on the dregs from the pitcher of martinis she had made earlier. The candles she had placed near the fireplace were now molten globs in their dishes.

By ten-thirty she had uncorked the first bottle of white wine and tipped almost half of it into her glass. After every swallow, she saluted Jace with another imaginary but graphic name.

By eleven that night she was skunk drunk and had cried herself to sleep on the couch. Her robe was half-belted, her apron jauntily covered one hip and her high-heeled shoes dangled from crimson toes.

MORNING CAME TOO QUICKLY for April. She opened one eye, moaned and rolled over. But the sunlight wouldn't go away. It cheerfully poured into the room to spread across her pillow. She groaned and slugged the pillow in her anger, only to feel the stiffness of paper.

It took five minutes to force her eyes into focusing on the broad scrawl. It took another five to decipher the message.

Put you to bed at two. See you this evening at seven. Can't wait to see how well you wear your head today. Two aspirin and glass of water on night table.

All my love,
Jace

She read it again. Then again. Her hair hurt as it bristled up the slim cord of her neck. Not one word about why he was late last night or that he was sorry!

She sat up, her anger forcing her into activity until she felt the pit of her stomach clenching, then turning over upside down in defiance of her movement.

"Ugh," she groaned again, not quite sure whether she should hold her head or her stomach. The decision was taken out of her hands. Standing on wobbly legs and suddenly wishing her bed were closer to the bathroom, she held both, barely making it to the toilet in time.

It took more than an hour for April to get showered and dressed and find her car. She had stood under the shower nozzle for nearly twenty minutes in an attempt to cleanse the feeling that death was imminent. The car was another matter. She forgot she had parked it in the garage and walked the length of the entire driveway twice before remembering. And she cursed Jace with every jarring step. If it hadn't been for him she would be cheerful and happy this morning. Instead she was suffering for his actions. Well...their actions. Well...her actions. But it was still his fault!

The car hit every small pothole in the road, and the curves seemed more treacherous than ever before, swaying her stomach back and forth with each small movement. When she finally jammed on the brakes in the parking lot, her stomach jammed, too.

Sam took one look at her and grinned. "Coffee, lots of cream and sugar. Coming up."

"Don't scream, Sam. I'm right here," she muttered, walking stiffly past his desk and into her own office. She sat down and tried to focus her eyes, staring at the large desk blotter in front of her, but it still took several minutes for the small pink telephone message slip to register on her more-than-foggy brain. In Jean's handwriting—the part-time girl they had just hired—was a clean, crisp note:

Mr. Sullivan's secretary called. He won't be home until late because he must meet with the script-writers. He's sorry, but it can't be helped.

The telephone call had been logged in at four twenty-five, fifteen minutes after she had left the office.

When Sam walked in, a cup of coffee in his hand, April held out the note to him. "Fire her," was all she said before gulping down the hot brew.

Sam read the note, then looked at April, his dark brows raised in question. "For this?"

"Yes."

"Why? She's only been here two weeks. She still has a lot to learn."

"What kind of office clerk would leave a message like this on my desk when it's obvious I should have been called at home? Only an incompetent one—that's what kind!" Her voice raised in anger. Glimpses of herself as she lay sprawled on the couch for Jace to find flashed through her mind, embarrassing her even more.

But somewhere in the pounding of her head, reason forced itself forward. Before Sam could even begin to calm her down, she realized just how stupid her reaction was and continued, "So I think she ought to be reprimanded by you and told the proper procedure for the future." She grinned sheepishly, recognizing his knowing look.

"Right, boss. I'll do that as soon as she comes in," he said, barely succeeding in his attempt to keep a straight face. "I gather that Jace didn't come home until late last night, and you were all ready to show off your newfound domesticity?"

"Something like that," she hedged, unwilling to remember the idiot she must have made of herself last night. This morning her apron was on the floor along with her robe. Her shoes were scattered, one on the floor of the living room, the other in the large entryway. She must have been a sight to behold! A dull red blush tinged her cheeks and neck. Jace must have thought she was crazy, and at a time when she was trying to show him how indispensable she was! Damn the secretary! Damn Jace for ruining her plans! Damn her for being drunk! That last thought kept her blush apparent.

Sam saw it and knew it was time to retreat. He did so. Quietly.

By midmorning she was feeling slightly better. Grimly realizing she wasn't going to die and therefore had to work, she settled for initialing and passing papers to the part-time girls while sipping on the 7-Up Sam kept handing her. Sam had ordered a light lunch for her, and it, too, had gone a long way in helping her stomach settle down to a low rumble.

Aspirin had aided her belief that she just might live through this, and Sam's surreptitious looks made her understand that she might have made a fool out of herself but she hadn't done anything irreparable, at least as far as Sam was concerned. Jace was another matter. How was she going to handle this?

When Jace called, she was ready.

"How are you feeling?" His voice was tinged with amusement.

"Fine," she answered brightly.

"When I came home last night, you were out for the count. What happened?"

"Oh, I had one-too-many martinis. I've never done it before, so I wouldn't dwell on it too much."

"Martinis, too? I found an empty wine bottle."

"Did you?" she asked innocently. "Perhaps it evaporated during the evening. I uncorked it before I knew you wouldn't be home for dinner." Her hand clenched. That was a dumb answer!

His chuckling echoed in her ears. Apparently he thought so, as well, but he didn't seem inclined to pursue the matter. "Did you get my message?"

"Oh, yes," she replied breezily. Not for anything in the world would she let him know she had made a fool of herself over him. The less he knew, the better off she was!

"Then how come you called the studio? Didn't you trust me?" His voice held a teasing note. He knew she had always hated talking to the bodiless voices on the other end before she could get through to him. Consequently she never called unless she had to.

"My secretary was late in giving me the message, so when I called, I didn't know if you had driven that darn car of yours off the canyon road or if you had another date." She shouldn't have said that! It sounded like a jealous girlfriend. She crossed her fingers, hoping he wouldn't notice the slip. Her luck was with her—bad, as usual. . . .

"If I have another date, Flynn, you'll be the first to know. I promise," was his answer, deep throated and sensual. Despite the decrepitness of her frail body, her spine shivered with his voice.

"Well, that's good enough for me," she said brightly. It wasn't, but she wouldn't admit it. *I'll get you, Mr. Sullivan, or I'll die trying!* This morning she thought she had died. Or maybe she wished she had! She still couldn't think straight. Never again would she touch a drink.

"Will you be home early tonight?" he asked softly, as if cupping the phone for privacy.

"Yes, I think so."

"Good. I'll get out of here as fast as I can. Maybe we can have a few drinks on the patio and watch the sunset. Then we'll curl up in front of the fireplace and see what happens."

The idea of drinks made her gag, but she wouldn't let him know for the world. She gulped down bile. "Sounds romantic, Mr. Sullivan." She thought of using his broad chest covered with dark, curly hair as a pillow; of his arms, so big and strong, holding her with restrained gentleness and his lips barely brushing her temple. Her breath became shorter; her heart thumped against her ribs. Suddenly she didn't feel so bad anymore.

"Good. Hold that thought," was his answer before he hung up.

The rest of the day perked up for April. Sam left early for class, having properly chastised the new girl in the office. At least he said he did, but Jean looked awfully happy to April's jaded eyes. Somehow she got the impression that Sam's meaning of the word "chastise" and hers didn't coincide.

Sam was a sucker for any pretty girl, always ready to defend and champion but never staying around any one girl long enough to forge a lasting relationship. April grinned. Someday someone was going to catch him, and when she did, April wanted to be around to see his struggling with the net. It would be nice to have the last laugh after the fiasco of the past week!

It wasn't until the end of the day that Jace called again, asking April to attend a party that night.

"I wouldn't go except that most of the cast will be there, along with some publicity people. It's a command performance. But I don't want to go by myself. I'd be bored to death," he said, sounding more exhausted than she was. Her heart went out to him. "There's even supposed to be some surprise guest!" he told her disgustedly. He hated those types of phony Hollywood parties. Everyone in the business went to them because they were supposed to, not because they wanted to. She and Jace hadn't attended a half dozen ever since they'd been together. Jace's idea of privacy was exactly that: *privacy*. Almost all of Hollywood didn't even know that Jace was already spoken for . . . in a manner of speaking.

"Of course I'll be there," she answered soothingly. She was even less fond of them than he was, but this was her turn to prove how supportive and wifely she could be. After all, wasn't it equivalent to a wife attending a company party? She hoped she was right. All this effort shouldn't go for nought.

HER BLACK CREPE DRESS was puritanically high necked and long sleeved. It wasn't until she turned around that anyone would notice the softly draped material that exposed her entire length of back. Her earrings were long loops of silver chain that brushed her shoulders every time she moved her head. Her hair was brushed forward to frame her ivory skin and blue eyes, instead of the more casual style she usually wore. Silver-strapped evening sandals with a bag to match completed her outfit.

She checked herself in the mirror, smiling at the image, pretending she was laughing at a joke. Good. She looked as sophisticated as she could with what she had to work with. She frowned. Why did she have to look like an updated version of Doris Day, when she really wanted to be Marilyn Monroe? She puckered her lips at the mirror. Instead of looking sexy, she looked as if she had just sucked a lemon. So much for sensual. . . .

The party was on Mulholland Drive. She had told Jace she would meet him there rather than have him drive back to get her. They could always park her car at the office later and he could take her to work again in the morning.

As she fitted her key into the front door to lock it, the phone began to ring. Cursing under her breath she ran in, almost tripping over her own high heels as she dashed across the entry hall and grabbed for the phone.

"Flynn? Where the hell are you?" Jace's voice snapped over the line, irritation lacing every word.

"I was just on my way out the door when you called. Where do you think I am?" she snapped back, equally irritated.

"I thought I said 'early.'"

"You did. Only my office and I have a different idea of 'early' than you do!" So much for acting the loving corporate wife.

She could hear his weary sigh on the other end, and suddenly her anger evaporated. He was obviously missing her. Her heart warmed on that thought.

"Flynn, be prepared." His voice was low, practically muffled by the closeness of the receiver. "My mother is here and she wants to meet you."

The phone turned to ice in her hands. His mother? He *hated* his mother! He had told April time and time again just how rotten it was that his mother had arranged for him to be raised by anyone and everyone, as long as she could continue with her career!

"Flynn?" Jace's voice jolted her back to the present.

"I'm here. Well, that's very nice. I'm looking forward to it," she said weakly.

"Nice, my foot! She wants to see if she can get something from you or me—I'd bet my career on it! I don't know what she's up to, but be careful. She's sneaky."

"Then why don't you just ignore her? That shouldn't be too hard. You've done that ever since I've known you."

"Because this place is crawling with press, and they'd love nothing better than to find out we're fighting. It would be in every rag in the country by morning. I can do without having my life exposed in black and white, thank you." His voice was sharp, crisp and laced with just enough dread to keep the edge off April's temper.

"Okay. I'll be there as fast as I can," she reassured him before hanging up. Poor darling. . . .

It was a perfect night for an outdoor party. No smog, just lots of beautiful stars and a midnight-blue velvet sky.

An attendant was outside the home, parking cars and giving tickets in exchange for the keys. She couldn't begin to understand where he would wedge another car, but hers was not to reason why.

A live combo was playing out on the patio from the sound of it. Carefully hidden lights in front and brilliant light coming from the back patio made the night look like day. The view, even from the front of the house, was awe-inspiring. All of Los Angeles lay at the foot of the hill, spread out like a magic carpet of light and dark patterns.

The front door was open and she walked in, her eyes darting around the room to find her poor Jace. As on edge as he was on the phone, she knew he'd probably be looking for her, needing her to help him keep his temper in line. He would see her and stay by her all night, not wanting to face this crowd of sharks alone. And she would help him do his duty admirably, be his rock in time of trouble. After all, what were corporate wives for?

As soon as she spotted him, she wished she hadn't. She could feel even her ears heat up as she watched the scene before her. His leading lady, Sandra Tanner, was draped on his arm and shoulder, a smile painted on her lovely full lips that would have made the Cheshire Cat jealous. Her dress was virgin white with seeded pearls sewn in strategic places, subtly pointing out all the curves that a quick glance might have missed. The long skirt was slit on both sides, so that in case eyes missed one slim length of leg, they could glimpse the other. Photographers' cameras clicked picture after picture of the two of them, until someone—April thought it was the producer—finally spoke up.

"Okay, guys, that's enough. After all, this is a party, not a publicity campaign!" He laughed in a congenial voice that seemed to be a trademark of the public-relations department.

Everyone laughed, knowing he lied. This was a pre-publicity party for the movie, one of the best ways to promote a light romantic comedy, and there was no doubt about it.

And Jace and Sandra Tanner seemed more than happy to oblige the press.

April seethed. She stood in the entryway that was three steps up from the large combination den and game room, and fumed. Did he have to look so happy about that girl panting down his neck? Sandra gazed into his eyes in adoration, and he didn't seem to mind at all. April's eyes narrowed as she looked at Sandra once more.

There was no competing with the bright, younger, beautiful movie star in her slinky designer dress. To compete they had to be on some type of equal footing, and no one could accuse them of that.

April straightened her spine, mentally preparing herself for battle. It would be a fight to the finish between herself as Mary Poppins and Sandra Tanner as a petite Marilyn Monroe, with the prize being Jace as Rhett Butler. And somehow, even if she had to use black magic, she'd win. But she wouldn't go to battle vying with Sandra Tanner for broad-shoulder space. Oh, no. She'd do it her way. . . .

Plastering what she hoped was a seductive and secretive smile on her face, she gracefully walked down the stairs, her head now turned to take in the many men watching her from the safety of the large, curving bar in the far corner. Truthfully she wasn't sure they were looking at her or just waiting for someone else to appear, but at this point she didn't care, either. She aimed toward them, her stomach revolting at the thought of a drink, but her mind screaming at her, telling her to turn her back on the scene by the fireplace.

"Can I get you something, sweetheart?" one of the men asked, and she smiled again.

"Yes, I'd love a, a . . . ." She couldn't form the word 'drink.' Last night was still too recent. "A glass of sparkling water with a twist of lime."

Brows went up all across the bar, but one of the gentlemen ordered her the drink she had requested. Once he put the drink in April's hand, he skillfully stepped in front of her, blocking her retreat toward Jace.

"Do you know Rolph well?"

So this was going to be cocktail-conversation time. "No, I've never met him," she said honestly, sipping on her drink and hoping her stomach wouldn't reject it.

"Oh? Then how come you're here?"

"At the request of a friend," she hedged, wondering why she was there herself. She could be home with a bottle of aspirin and a hot shower, reading a perfectly lovely, dull law book.

The man stared at her, his brown eyes half-closed. Then a knowing smile came slowly over his face. "You're one of Abe's girls, aren't you?"

"Nope," she answered, turning her back on him, preparing to walk away. Who was 'Rolph'? Better still, who was 'Abe'? Two wolf whistles assaulted her ears, and she realized that instead of snubbing the man, she had incited him. He thought the back of her dress was an invitation for more intimacy.

"Oh, honey. Don't leave yet. I have to find out what sign you're under. Who knows? We might be compatible."

She looked over her shoulder, determined to get the last word. "I only believe in Chinese astrology and I'm the sign of the cat. Don't tell me. I bet you're a rat, aren't you?"

The laughter from the men crowding the bar was loud as April walked away, swaying her hips just slightly. One victory swallowed, another to go.

She didn't have long to wait. About five seconds and three steps across the room, and Jace was standing in front of her, a dark scowl on his face. His look told her of his anger, but her stomach was in no mood to tighten at his possessiveness. After all, she had come here at his invitation just to watch that damn act of his with Sandra on his arm. He had finally left Sandra's side, only April hadn't noticed it until he confronted her.

"It's about time you got here." He looked down at her, purposely taking her arm and glaring, making it plain to the men still standing at the bar that she was his and no one else's.

"I've been here for a while, but you were too busy to notice." Just for spite she glanced over her shoulder and gave the man who had got her a drink a very sexy mew. He looked back at her, apparently confused.

"Then why didn't you make me notice?" His look was more grim than a grin.

"I just finished telling that man I'm a cat. That doesn't mean I was raised in an alley." Her nose was raised daintily in the air; her voice was cool, with just the right touch of disdain. His scowl grew deeper.

"No, but usually when you want something, Flynn, you go after it," was his angry reply. "I was only fifteen steps away."

"I didn't notice."

Suddenly he relaxed. "It can't be both, my Flynn. First you said I looked busy, and now you're telling me you didn't notice. Which was it?"

She struggled to continue her anger, but she finally had to smile reluctantly in response. "Who's the lawyer here, anyway?"

"You are," he answered, reassured by her smile and the twinkle in her eyes that she was caught in her lie. He took her arm in a firmer clasp and led her out to the patio. The band was playing in one corner, while people were scattered about, conversing. "And I hope you have a sharp mind tonight, Flynn." Suddenly his voice became hard, his grip stronger. "My mother's decided to come out of hiding—or 'retirement,' as she calls it—and grace the press with her company. She's been living in the south of France with some count for the past four years and thinks it's time to get in touch again. She's also heard about you and me and that we've been living together. She thinks it's her motherly duty to meet you." His voice was leaden with satire. He wasn't even pretending to smile any more.

"How nice."

"Not really. I'd call it a long-overdue-case-of-motherhood attack if I were eight or ten years old, but I'm not. She wants something." His voice was heavily laced with cynicism. "But the press is here, and so we play her game. For now."

April looked up at him as he ushered her toward the other side of the pool. He had spoken about his mother on rare occasions, and nothing he had to say had been good. She was a famous actress who had been married as many times as most women change clothes. Jace was her only offspring, and he had been raised by boarding schools and governesses all his life.

April had the opinion that his mother was the real reason he was so against marriage. From what she had heard, he had every right to be. She was also his reason for not having children, having been raised the haphazard way he had been. April had the feeling that half the problems she had in talking Jace into marriage could be laid in his mother's lap. She took a deep breath. This should prove interesting, if not enlightening.

He slowly walked her around the pool, aiming toward a small group of people sitting in lawn chairs at the back of the sloping garden. April spotted her immediately. The woman Jace was aiming her toward was beautiful, even more beautiful in person than the photos April had seen of her. Long black hair pulled back and intricately knotted at her nape showed off a slim, straight, wrinkleless neck that most ballerinas would envy. Jet-black brows gently arched above sea-green eyes, giving her high cheekbones even more prominence. Erica Sullivan was still as lovely today as when she had made movies several years ago.

She was seated in a padded lawn chair, ankles crossed and hands gracefully relaxed on her lap. It could just as easily have been a throne. Her head was tilted up as she chuckled at something the young man bending over her was saying.

She glanced over to see Jace leading April toward her and allowed her dramatically slanted eyes to widen in both delight and surprise. April was amazed at how young she looked. Not only was she beautiful, but her face was so open in its genuine happiness to see Jace that she had a hard time melding her impression of his mother with the real thing.

"There you are!" she exclaimed huskily, reaching for Jace's hand. He gave it reluctantly. "I knew you'd be back. I just didn't expect you to be gone so long, darling."

Jace stiffened. "As you well know, it's business first, Erica. I had to pose for some publicity shots." He turned toward April, his hand releasing hers only to tighten on her waist. "April Flynn, I'd like you to meet Erica Sullivan. Erica, Flynn."

"'Flynn,'" the older woman mused as she took April's hand in hers. "It sounds like an old World War Two flying ace. Really, Jace, couldn't you call the woman by her first name? I understand you two have become quite an item for the past several years, so you might as well own up publicly to knowing her."

"Jace is one of the few people who knows me well enough to call me 'Flynn,' Mrs. Sullivan." April's voice was low but very clear, not brooking argument but neither begging at feet. "As for being an 'item,' I doubt if half the people at this party know that Jace and I are...are together."

"Oh, dear." Erica took another, closer look at the woman her son had chosen, her glance encompassing April from head to toe. "I fear I've already got off on the wrong foot. Please forgive my blunder. Jace makes me as nervous to be around as I seem to make him. I did so want us to be friends."

A quick glance at Jace made April smile. He looked as if he could easily throttle his mother. "I'm sure neither of us will allow a little name to get in the way of our friendship," April said soothingly. Whose name might hinder that friendship, she couldn't say. But Fight Fire with Fire was the motto of the day. All her nerves were tuned to Erica. She couldn't figure out what Jace's mother wanted from her, but she was sure she wanted something. Jace had been right about that. It was apparent in her moves and voice.

"Oh, good." Erica smiled at April, then at Jace, before turning to her escort. "John, darling, please fill my glass with some of that good whiskey, would you? Straight, dear, no ice," she ordered before turning back to April and motioning to another chair. "Come sit for a while, April, and tell me about yourself." She patted the chair cushion next to her. "I'm sorry we haven't had a chance to meet before, although I've heard so many interesting things about you." Her laughter lilted through the air. "And I'm sure you've heard about me. Jace used to be very vocal about me in his early days, although I'm told that he's now silent on the subject of his mother."

Jace's scowl got deeper and blacker, if that was possible. April smiled sweetly and sat down as she had been beckoned. Right now she wasn't that thrilled with Jace that she would do exactly what he wanted. He had been far too busy earlier to notice her, so if he didn't like her actions now, he could always keep company with that sexy siren. As soon as she realized what she just thought, she retracted the idea. Was she crazy? One should never trail bait in front of a hungry shark unless one meant business!

Erica looked up at her son, exasperation clear on her beautifully unlined face. "Jace, dear, either sit down or go away. I refuse to crane my neck only to watch you scowl."

"But I've learned to do it so well when you're around, Erica. Wouldn't you miss it?" His answer was flip, but his growl showed his aggravation.

"No," his mother snapped. "Now go away for a while and let me talk to April. After all, I understand that you've been together for three years, so you should know what she's like by now. I promise that I've had my fill to eat today. I won't devour your latest love."

"Only," April said quietly, and both mother and son stared at her in surprise. "Only love," she explained patiently.

"Why, my dear, how do you know that?" Erica's perfectly arched brows rose, and her eyes widened.

"Because if I didn't, I wouldn't be here. One at a time is all that's necessary. Any more is gluttony," she answered primly, but with enough self-assurance that both Jace and Erica were taken aback.

Jace chuckled first, his dark-brown eyes glowing with that magic light April loved so well. Appreciation of her quickness of mind was also in his eyes, and she basked in it. One answer down and one hundred to go.

"In that case, since Flynn trusts me, I'll leave you two alone." His smile was replaced with a scowl as he looked back in warning at his mother. "But only for a little while. Flynn and I aren't staying much longer."

Erica sighed in exasperation. "I understand, Jace. Now run along and make your agent happy by grinning a lot. Everyone loves your dimples. Go use them."

April watched Jace walk around the side of the pool, making his way back into the center of the party. She had thought she could handle his mother, but now that they were suddenly alone, doubts assailed her. She had a million questions to ask, but one stood out: what did the woman want with her?

"Now that the men are finally gone, perhaps we can relax and have a decent conversation. They're so distracting, don't you think?" Erica smiled, and once more April realized just what a beautiful woman she was. No one would guess her age to be over forty. Yet April knew that just by the virtue of numbers, she had to be closer to sixty.

"Why did you want to speak to me privately, Mrs. Sullivan?" Might as well grab the bull by the horns, she thought with a premonition of disaster. April's voice was quiet, her eyes direct, and she was surprised to see that her composure seemed to make the other woman jittery.

"Well, I had heard that you've been living with my son for the past three years, and I wanted to know what kind of a woman could hold his interest all that time. Jace has never been known to have any relationship last very long. Other than his nanny, who died eight years ago, he doesn't have a good record where the women in his life are concerned." Her eyes stared out at the darkness before resting once more on April.

"His father passed away just five years after Jace was born, but he was the same way—never building on a relationship, only using it until the next one came along." The older woman hesitated for a moment, her gaze turning inward. "I often thought we would make it together despite his sordid past. I was going to be the woman to change him. And I might have, if he hadn't crashed into the side of a mountain on his way back to me from the Swiss Alps. He was a very charming man. Jace looks just like him. . . ." Her voice dwindled off, and she seemed to shake herself mentally out of her reverie. "So now Jace is doing the same thing, and you seem to be the object of his affection. That makes you the exception and the exceptional, my dear. You must be very special—"

April smiled and finished the sentence for her. "Or he's in his dotage?"

A low lilting laugh again filled the air. "Oh, never that! Why, if he got any older, then I'd have to, too! And I'm not ready for that yet." Erica chuckled before her piercing green eyes locked with April's once more. "But tell me, does the length of your relationship with Jace mean there is marriage in the future?"

"Why?" Despite the fact that her heart pace stepped up at her words, April's eyes never left Erica's face. Her stare was as direct as her question.

"I just thought that the mother ought to be the first to know." She shrugged elegantly, but for just a moment, April could see the hurt in her eyes. "No matter how Jace and I react to each other, I am his mother."

"Then why ask me? Why not ask Jace?"

"Because Jace sometimes forgets who brought him into the world. I may have my faults, April, but I did the best I could with what I had to work with at the time. I made sure that he had everything he needed. I loved him and I cared for him. He was my pride and joy. But I didn't have the time in those days to devote to raising a child. I had to earn a living. Jace's father left no legacy except Jace himself and a mountain of bills. I had a career that demanded almost all my time and energy, and it was even harder to be a success back then." Erica looked down at her hands, her voice low and slightly uneven. "I just don't want to be made to look like a fool, and his announcing a wedding without telling me would make me appear silly to the press and give the gossips something else to pin on my already-long list of misdeeds."

April stared out at the pool. There was still something that she was missing, some small piece of the puzzle, and she couldn't put her finger on it. Was the woman acting, or was she telling the truth? She looked at Erica again, her attorney's instincts alive and throbbing. She still couldn't tell.

After a long silence April spoke. "I'm sorry. I didn't mean to seem uncaring. But I think you still need to talk to Jace about his personal life." She leaned back in her chair. She was suddenly bone tired, and her stomach was acting up again.

"I gather, then, that the subject of marriage hasn't been discussed between you two," Erica said, her voice clearly showing her disappointment.

It was time to stop the chitchat and get to the heart of things. "Why?" April asked. "What was it you wanted me to help you with that you felt I would be better able to do as a wife?" She had a few thoughts on the subject herself, but she wasn't about to go into that with Jace's mother!

Erica smiled, but her eyes showed her surprise. "Am I that transparent?"

"Not really, but it stands to reason that if you're pushing for marriage, you must have a reason. I'm trying to understand that reason."

"It must be your attorney's training, but you're right. Yet marriage alone wouldn't be a help." Erica turned in her chair, leaning toward April eagerly as she began to speak. "You see, there's a script I'm dying to do. It's perfect for me—the role of a woman who's neither the love interest nor the 'mother' type. Only the studio, which happens to own this piece, wants Jace to play the part of the younger brother. They think he'll sell tickets and it would be a guaranteed hit. I think he'd be wonderful in it, too, but for different reasons. It's a dramatic, meaty role and one that he would be able to handle well. He has great depth of feeling. It would showcase his dramatic talent so well."

"Has he been asked?"

"Yes. He even has the script, but according to his agent, he hasn't read it yet. Of course, he doesn't know it's the same movie I want to make."

"And you want me to see that he reads it and says yes." April's heart went down to her feet. She had never interfered with Jace's career and wasn't about to begin now, but if the role was good . . . .

"I only want you to make sure he reads it," Erica corrected gently. "That's all. He has to know the role would be wonderful for him, or all the money in the world wouldn't force him to do it."

"Excuse me, Mrs. Sullivan, but I think I'm missing something. Jace reads all the scripts and decides for himself whether he thinks they're right for him. When he reads that one, he'll either say yes or no, but he won't hedge. If you know we're close, then you should know I never interfere with his career judgments. Why do you need me?"

"I'm just afraid that if he hears I might be playing the part of his older sister before he reads it, then he'll be prejudiced against it. I'm asking for a fair reading. That's all. The name of the script is *Goodbye, Spring,* and I know he received it sometime this past month."

April gave a heavy sigh. "I'll see what I can do," she said reluctantly, promising herself she would interfere as little as possible.

"No, you won't, April." Jace's voice growled from the darkness. They both looked up to find him, drink in hand, next to April's chair. "Remember the deal we made? We don't meddle in each other's careers." He stepped onto the pavement of the pool from the shadowed garden. "If my mother is having a problem getting another of her 'comebacks' off the ground, I suggest she look to her own agent and publicity man. Mine are concerned only with my career, not hers, thank God."

With a stare that would have frozen the balmy breezes, he stalked off, walking back toward the house again. April stared after him, watching him shrug others off as he made his way to the front door. Her heart hit her toes as she realized he was leaving. But what was worse was that he believed she had been trying to interfere with his career and relationship with his mother.

Erica cleared her throat. "I'm sorry, April. I certainly didn't mean to come between you and Jace," she said sadly, her hand reaching out to pat April's numb arm. In fact, all of April was numb. She couldn't believe he was so insensitive to her!

"That's all right," April said absently, her mind already on the next confrontation with Jace.

"No, I should have known Jace would react that way. He's got an enormous amount of hate in him. I had thought it had died down, but . . . ."

April stood, anxious to get away. "Please don't worry. Everything will be fine," she said reassuringly, at the same time trying to keep her heartbeat below double time. "I hope I see you again, Mrs. Sullivan. Goodbye."

The older woman watched her walk away, her parting words still on her lips.

4

How HAD SHE GOT so involved in what clearly wasn't any of her business? April's steps clicked on the concrete of the patio as she dodged the small groups of people who stood and chatted.

Why, after three years of living with him, would Jace honestly believe she was conspiring against him? Didn't he know her better than that?

There were no answers. Just a building anger.

It took her another fifteen minutes to find her purse and make her way through the crowd that had gathered around the stairway. When she reached the door, the group that was entering was far larger than the group leaving, which was her, and she had to wait for nearly half an hour before the parking attendants could even find her car, let alone move all the others to get to it! By the time she slid behind the wheel her temper was at full tilt.

Driving home alone, she cursed under her breath all the way. He had some nerve! After all, *he* had been the one who'd eavesdropped, only hearing the tail end of a very long conversation! He hadn't even asked for an explanation of her reply. Who did he think he was? Mr. Wonderful? She ignored the answer to that.

When she reached their home, April placed her hand on the hood of Jace's Alfa. From the coolness of it she knew he had been home for a long time. She opened the front door and walked in, slamming it behind her. Her motions were agitated, expressive of her state of mind. Stomping through the entryway to make sure he heard her, she threw her keys and purse on the couch in the living room, her anger and fear still teetering like a seesaw. As she had driven home, her mind had turned somersaults until she was confused and angry with both mother and son.

How dared they put her in this position! She wasn't a worm to be put between a rock and a hard place! She was too angry to remember the fact that he had never been anything but considerate with her before. His three years of tenderness were wiped out in three minutes of pure bullheadedness!

April stepped back into the hallway, flipping on lights as she went. Jace was home but not in the bedroom. Nor was he in the kitchen or living room. Apparently he had not bothered to turn on the outside lights or interior music, or cared to let her know he was home. The house was deadly quiet. Then, very softly, came the sound of lapping water. She glanced down. His suit jacket was on the floor. Three feet farther down the hall and toward the dining room was his tie. Farther still was his shirt.

"Ah, so. He's playing the role of Hansel," she murmured to herself, still not quite ready to admit she was relieved to know where he was and what he was doing. "Then he must want me to play Gretel." Obviously he had gone for a swim. All she had to do

was follow the dropped clothing and she'd find him in
no time. Then she could give him a good piece of her
mind!

The sliding back door was open, the drapes pulled
aside so she could see the lights of the courtyard. Jace
was swimming the length of the pool, his strokes even,
his kick small but propelling. Her eyes alighted on the
last puddle of clothing—his underwear—near the
pool's edge. Her heart skipped a beat. He hadn't
bothered to change into a suit. He was naked.

As much as she tried to keep a tenacious hold on her
anger, it didn't work. Pity for him and the tenuous
relationship he had with his mother and desire to
cleave him to her pushed her anger away.

She walked to the edge of the pool and watched his
strokes more closely. He acknowledged her presence
by giving her a hard stare, then continued swimming.
Neither of them said a word.

She smiled, suddenly understanding a little of his
frustration. He was angry, but he was also aroused, if
the shadows of the lightly heated water revealed what
she thought they did. With slow deliberation she
began unzipping her black dress. When it slithered to
the concrete to join his clothes, she gracefully slipped
out of her panties.

Jace rolled on his back, his strokes keeping an even
rhythm, but his eyes were glued to her. The dark hair on
his chest glistened like black and silver diamonds in the
water. His lungs heaved with breath; his features were
taut and fine. The air crackled with wire-tight tension.
April stood poised on her toes at the edge of the pool,
her arms raised above her head. Then, with perfect

symmetry born of practice, she dove into the water.

When she came up for air, Jace was continuing his stroke, but his eyes had followed her trail. She began swimming to his rhythm, remaining only a foot or so away from his side as they both exorcised the ghosts that had driven them into the pool in the first place. Only the sound of the disturbed water and their own breathing stirred the night air.

They paced for three laps, then four, then five. Finally April slowed, her muscles gradually releasing her from the tension that had brought her there. Jace lessened his pace, automatically keeping the tempo. When she finally stopped to catch her breath by the shallow steps that led up and out, so did he.

Leaning against the side, her head thrown back, her arms perched on the steps just below water level, she allowed her legs to float in front of her.

"Jace . . ." she began, only to stop. She didn't know what to say. She knew he was hurt enough to be so furious as to lose the tenderness they usually communicated to each other. Had she ruined it between them? Did he really think she had betrayed him in favor of his mother? Did he believe that, or was he just angry with his mother? How could she explain her own confused emotions right now? Her blue eyes glittered brightly in the underwater light, showing him more than her words just how she felt.

"Sh," he said, laying a finger over her parted lips, then rubbing it lightly back and forth as if applying a soothing balm. Her heartbeat, which had been slowing, began revving again. His very touch made her feel warm all over.

"Later. Not now." They stared into each other's eyes, both silently saying more then than they had said all night. Her teeth lightly captured his finger and took it into her mouth, her tongue tracing the shape of it, sucking gently as she watched the consequence of her actions on his face. He closed his eyes with the intensity of his feelings. Then, slowly, with the power of a burst of sunrise, he smiled.

Relief almost smothered her with its brilliant intensity.

"Do you understand?" she whispered.

Those brown, piercing eyes locked with hers, sending her definite signals she couldn't ignore. She searched his face for more, seeing only the tenderness of his look. He nodded. "I think so."

"Then will you kiss me?"

His smile became even brighter, almost breaking her heart with the sweetness of it. "And make it better?"

It was her turn to nod. She swallowed the large lump in her throat. "I hurt so much," she said.

Then it was his turn to soothe. His dark head lowered, poising over one breast. Anticipation made her catch her breath. His tongue came out to exact payment of her words, lapping the sensitive tip before taking the bud in his mouth and laving it with all his attention.

She moaned, one hand coming up to touch the hardness of his haired chest. Her body was floating in the water and only his mouth kept her buoyant. His hands caressed all her flesh as she drifted in front of him, moving over her as if he were sculpting a perfect replica of her body. Strange, yet not-so-strange sensations filled her, spreading throughout her being as he continued to taunt her willing form with his almost nearness.

His lips left her breast only to capture her mouth, giving her his breath in exchange for the exquisite torture he had put her through. A deep moan escaped her throat, telling him more than words what her reaction to his tender touch was.

Her hands reached around his neck and clasped him to her, needing to feel the touch of skin against skin. She pressed against him, eager to feel his need and have him know hers, experience that wonderful, familiar pressure building as his hard body molded itself to hers. He pulled her toward him as if she were his anchor, and she reveled in the pressure he exerted.

Her thoughts careened around, only to return without anything but feelings wrapped together to make sensations too wonderful to ignore. She was breathless with the power that surged through him, and her head began to spin with the need that only he aroused. Did he know how she felt in the circle of his arms? She pressed closer to let him understand without words. She loved him. She loved him so. . . .

He slid her body upright against his and, with passion born of intense need, thrust himself into her, his hands tightening as they left her waist and circled her back to keep the contact as close as he could.

A gasp left both their parted lips before April reached up to claim the sides of his head and bring it down to her lips, kissing him with all the pent-up love she had inside her.

It was a powerful, desperate kind of lovemaking that only came occasionally and was all the more needed for its elemental closeness. They were nowhere, half floating, half standing in the middle of the universe.

Jace shuddered, his control completely gone. "No," he muttered, attempting to hold on to that small thread of restraint.

"Yes, Jace. Now!" she whispered urgently to him, and held tighter as her hands clasped the back of his straining neck. With one final thrust they were both on their way to that secret, special place only the other could guide them to.

Bodies sleek from the water were now warmed by their breath as they stood, forehead to forehead, and regained their composure. Jace's hands rested on her hips, while April's hands were still locked about his neck. Slowly they both began to smile. Jace tightened his grip slightly as he rubbed her from side to side, his smile widening with the deliciousness of the touch.

Finally April couldn't keep the words to herself any longer. "I love you, Jace Sullivan. With all my heart and soul, I love you."

"Come on," he said, raising his head. And he picked her up in his arms and strode up the pool steps with her, their wet bodies clinging. He walked across the patio and into the opened door.

"Jace," she whispered, her nails combing lightly through his hair, her eyes brilliantly alight with love for him. He stared straight ahead, his profile strong and tough and yet so very vulnerable. "Did you hear me? I said I love you."

"You'd better," he growled in a low voice, stopping only long enough to give her a deep, searching look. "I better not be the only one in this relationship that aches with the wonder of love. I couldn't stand that." Satisfied with what he saw on her face, he continued on to the bedroom.

The September night air cooled the heat their wanting had generated, and the water evaporated from them as they dried each other off with soft and hard skin-to-skin contact. They made love again, only this time slowly, tenderly, as if they both held fragile blossoms in their hands and were afraid to crush them.

When he joined with her, the blossoms burst into full bloom as they merged their deeply felt emotions into one beautiful flowering thought. They spoke with hands and sighs afterward, each understanding the other. There had been no hesitation in the giving and sharing. No holding back in the beauty they expressed at the hands of the other. It had been as perfect as it could get.

And then came blessed, wonderful peace. Legs and arms entwined, hands clasping flesh, heads close together, breathing in unison. April gave a soft sigh that was absorbed and returned by Jace. Their lovemaking had been a healing salve, and they slept away the small remainder of hurt left.

THURSDAY MORNING came too early. April burrowed beneath the covers, her eyes too tired to wake and enjoy the day . . . and Jace's good humor.

"Good morning, Sunshine! Wake up. Here's coffee." His voice seemed to boom in the air when all should be still. She groaned in resistance to the outside world. Last night she hadn't had one drink, but she was so tired all her eyes wanted to do was hide in sleep once more.

But he wouldn't let her. "Come on, you're due at the office in a few minutes," Jace said, prodding her.

She peeped her head out of the covers, opening one wary eye. "Really?"

He nodded, trying to hold in his smile and barely succeeding. She looked like a tousled child, an enchanting woman, and he loved her this way. Later, when she was dressed and on her way to work, she would look cool and in charge and sophisticated. The ultimate female attorney. But now she was the woman he adored, and his feelings showed in the tobacco-brown gleam in his eyes. This was the April Flynn whom he, and no one else, knew. It was his secret. He loved it.

"You now have fifteen minutes to shower and get dressed. Come on, gal." He gave a pat to her bottom encased in the sheets. "I can't always be the first one up and ready to face the world."

She stretched. "Why not? You do it so well."

He chuckled. Even coming out of a deep sleep, her mind was clicking right along.

"When I'm old and gray, you'd better be up before me and have my breakfast on the table. I want to enjoy my retirement, not wait on a snippy old attorney who still refuses to cope with more than a coffeepot in the kitchen."

"Dry up," she muttered as she scowled at the sunlight. Why did she have to be a night person? Count Dracula must have been a distant relative of hers.

Jace chuckled again, reading the basics of her thoughts. Instead of taking her in his arms and holding her close to the beat of his heart, he took a deep breath and gave her another slap on her well-blanketed rump. "Up! The day's a'wasting and I have to go to work!"

"Slave driver," she said between yawns, finally sitting up to survey with a jaundiced eye the beautiful sunny day. Why did everything have to be so *bright* in the mornings? Couldn't the day come gradually, kind of sneak up on her around ten or eleven in the morning?

She knew she had three new clients coming in today, and it wouldn't be right if the object of their appointment wasn't there to meet with them. She shook her head and forced her eyes to remain open. Suddenly she remembered the night before and her meeting with Jace's mother. As much as she felt sorry for the way Jace had been raised, she also felt sorry for his mother and the task she'd had of raising a small boy by herself. But there was no question as to where April's loyalties lay.

She wrapped her arms around her bent legs as she watched Jace move around the room. He was dressing. His hair was still damp from the shower. Black jeans outlined his neat rear and long, strong legs. He chose a shirt that contrasted well with his coloring—a rust-and-tan pullover.

"Jace?"

"Hmm?"

"About last night with your mother," she began, only to have him turn to her, the stormy look in his eyes telling her that her timing was all wrong.

"It's over. Now that you've met her, I don't want to discuss her. My mother and I were never close, but duty is done and you now know my roots. But from now on the subject is closed. All right?"

"No! It's not all right! I'm trying to apologize for what you thought you overhead, but why I should is beyond me! You were the one listening in the dark like some, some, Peeping Tom! I was just having a conversation!"

"Correction. You were trying to figure out a way to maneuver me because my mother played on your sympathy. I can understand that—she's a superb actress. But I thought you loved me enough not to be taken in by her. And I only heard the last part of your conversation. I was innocently returning with a drink for you, thinking you needed rescuing, when you really needed nothing from me," he said disgustedly. He pulled the shirt over his head and down his lean body. His face was expressionless as he continued. "But I know just how my mother manipulates people, so I understand your feelings."

"How?" she asked sweetly. "By reading my lips?" She exaggeratedly mouthed obscenities at him, receiving a small, "tut-tut," for her efforts that made her feel small and underlined her childishness.

Finally he faced her, hands placed on very masculine, trim hips. "Look. Whatever you agreed to do, just forget it. I take care of my own career and you take care of yours. Mothers and lovers stay out of it."

She swallowed back the words she wanted to spit out. "Lovers," indeed. Was that all she was? She tried a different, more open and vulnerable attack. "Can't we even discuss what happened last night?"

"No."

"You're impossible." She rested her head on her knees. When she looked up again he was staring at her. There was no anger in his eyes, only tenderness, and it was almost her undoing. She wanted to lift the blanket and invite him back into bed. She also wanted to hit him over the head with the nearest heavy object.

"See you tonight," he said huskily, obviously feeling much the same way she did.

"About six," she replied, her eyes following the line of his arms and chest, resting on the firm length of thigh and finally the slight rounding of his zipper. What a nice compact package he was! It was a shame he was so hardheaded!

"ANYTHING INTERESTING?" April asked Sam in a very uninterested voice.

"A Mrs. Judson wants an appointment to see you. She was sent over by Clair at the Halfway House. Clair says the woman might be ready to file for divorce, naming her own mother as a correspondent. It seems her husband prefers to be mothered rather than loved."

"Don't they all!" she muttered under her breath, knowing it wasn't true. It just felt good! "Set it up for this afternoon, if you can, Sam," she said with a sigh, sipping on the mug of coffee he handed her.

"I have some papers for you to sign, too. They're on Joanne's desk."

He peered at her again. There was no response to his words. "Okay. Now what's wrong? Yesterday you were celebrating a hangover and now you look as if you lost your best friend, except I know better, 'cause I'm right here." His dark-brown eyes, usually so full of fun, were narrowed, obviously contemplating what a wide range of moods she had shown lately.

April walked to the window and stared out. The sunshine was so bright the sky was a light, washed-out blue. People hurried to other offices on their way to work. "I don't know," she finally said. "What do wives do besides cook dinner and wash white loads of clothing pink?" She turned around, a small smile on her lips that didn't seem to reach her eyes. "I even tried to console his mother last night, and that fell through."

Sam whistled through his teeth. "Wow, you met Erica Sullivan? Is she as beautiful as everyone says?"

"Yes. More beautiful than I'll ever be if I had three plastic surgeries at once. And charming. And impatient. And wanting a comeback."

Sam's eyes lit with interest. "A comeback, huh? And who's supposed to play her leading man? Jace?"

"How did you know?"

He shrugged. "Just a lucky guess. Jace is top box office right now, and she'd aim for the best. What happened? Fireworks?"

"Fourth of July. Jace—" she swallowed hard "—Jace... overheard us talking and jumped to the wrong conclusion. I was trying to reassure Erica that

I'd talk to Jace only about reading the script, but he took it to mean I'd try to talk him into playing the part."

"Oh, boy. He must have loved that!" Sam's voice was thick with sarcasm.

"Apparently not. He won't even talk to me about it. He refuses to discuss his mother or his career." Her blue eyes stared up at Sam, and his heart went out to the misery he saw there. "Sam, I've never interfered, but somehow I've messed this one up, anyway. He won't even listen to me."

"Sounds like a typical husband."

"He's so angry."

"How angry?" Sam asked. "Angry enough to scream and yell at you? Angry enough to kick you out?"

"Well," April hedged, her mind suddenly replaying Jace's face as he'd made love to her in the pool last night.

Sam saw the look and read it correctly. "If that look means what I'm thinking it means, then Jace may be irritated, but he's certainly not angry," he said dryly.

April ignored that. "It sounds to me like the first step in breaking up," she said dourly, barely able to keep the tears at bay.

"No, if he wanted to do that, he'd come up with a better reason than a mother he already didn't like."

"You think so?" Her eyes begged him for a shred of hope.

"Definitely," Sam lied, crossing his fingers.

She brightened perceptibly. Heaving a deep sigh,

she smiled with her eyes for the first time. "In that case, I'll continue with my campaign. Tomorrow I need the whole day off. Think you can handle the office?"

"Sure, but what's up?"

"I'm cleaning house all day, cooking in the evening and playing wife at night," she said smugly.

"Sounds like the average day in the life of a housewife-to-be," Sam teased as he picked up the letters and placed them in front of her. "Read fast so I can get things working on this end. Most of them just need a comment or two. The rest of this mess the secretaries or I can answer."

Picking up her pen for notations, she grinned again. "Yes, sir." Suddenly she was thankful she had trained Sam in office procedure while waiting for him to get his degree. Now she'd be able to have a vacation. The training would prove invaluable not only for the month of October she was to be away, but now, when she couldn't seem to concentrate on her own rank-and-file work. She'd make it up to Sam when she returned from Oregon...if she went away at all. It seemed it was all up to Jace.

THE FOLLOWING MORNING, she watched Jace drive off down the winding canyon road. The house was quiet, the coffee fresh and she had all day to achieve her goal. First housecleaning and then dinner—which would be a replay of the one he'd missed.

By midafternoon April was wondering if she had grown new muscles in her slim body. Everything ached from more than energetic overuse. With a

Coke in one hand, she plopped down in the lawn chair and stared at the blue water of the pool.

Last night had been quiet and relaxed. Well, quiet, anyway. Jace and she had done the same things they always did, including smiling and teasing, but there was an element of wariness in both of them. When they had gone to bed early, he had held her in his arms and she had cuddled to him like a teddy bear. With light kiss on her forehead, he had gone quickly to sleep, breathing deeply and evenly enough to lull her into a false sense of security...at least for the night.

Was she wrong? Did he love her, or was she an answer to expediency? Was she handy to have around because she didn't usually interfere with his career or his habits? The look in Sandra Tanner's eyes the other night confirmed that she was crazy about Jace, too. April's hand tightened instinctively into a fist. Did Jace care? He hadn't seemed to, but, then, he was an actor....

She loved him so much that sometimes it hurt to acknowledge it. He was everything to her and she thought that he knew it, but she was never sure where she placed in his life. Was she first, second or third? Was she on his list of priorities at all? It was the not knowing that was killing her.

And was she doing the right thing in trying to get him to marry her? There was a pure streak of tradition in her that said it would be the only way she would be happy. She wanted to hold her head up, be proud of their relationship, not hear snickers from behind people's hands as they watched them dine, or walk or dance. From her standpoint it was the only thing that made sense. But from his...she didn't know.

He had been so bitter when she'd first met him. Marriages had broken up all around him, and the few couples that remained together did so only for tax purposes. Then, of course, there was his mother... but the biggest scar he bore was his aversion to marriage.

She slumped in the chair. How could one beat away the ghosts that had built up over a lifetime? She sat up. Could she show him that marriage *was* successful with the right people? But how? She slumped even more in the chair. They had few friends, they didn't know any good marriages and certainly none of her clients were good examples. If anything, over the past eight years she should have become as hardened against marriage as he was. California wasn't the best place to seek wedded bliss, if the statistics were anything to go by, especially in his profession.

In four weeks they would be leaving for their vacation. If he hadn't proposed by then, would she stick to her guns and call their arrangement off? The pain would be enormous, but, then, so would the failure to know where she stood in his life.

The timer she had set to let her know when her fifteen-minute break was over went off. With a confused mind, heavy heart and dragging feet, she moved back indoors. It was time to start dinner.

Her respect for housewives had risen a good eighty-five percent since she had begun this morning.

If they didn't find a new housekeeper soon, she would fade away from exhaustion. This was damn hard work! Jace had promised to call a domestic agency this week, but so far no interviews had been set up. A movie star had to be careful whom he hired. It had to be someone who would be stable—and tight-lipped to boot.

JACE GUNNED THE CAR ENGINE and began the ascent to the canyon road that led home. He changed gears automatically, his mind still on his problem: April Flynn.

He shouldn't have invited her to that press party, but he had needed her reassurance in that house of crazy people. He and Flynn were probably the only two there who weren't either swapping partners, smoking dope or popping pills. He shouldn't have got angry with her for being taken in by his bitch of a mother. He shouldn't have left her to drive home alone.

Then he went over the "shoulds." He should have tried to explain better his relationship with his mother. He should have been more understanding when April tried to discuss her. He should have taken her in his arms and kissed her breathless, which was what he wanted to do. He should have proposed to her—and if he hadn't wanted to save it for that perfect moment when they'd be alone at the cabin, he would have.

He made a sharp turn and gunned the engine again.

That party was the brunt of his dissatisfaction.

Sandra had decided to follow the publicity department's advice to the hilt and had played up to him as if she were the light in his eyes. And Flynn had seen it, just as he had. And just as he had, Flynn had guessed that the girl really was chasing after him. He wasn't sure how he could reassure her Sandra was just another co-star to him and Flynn was the real woman in his life, but he knew he had to.

If Flynn ever left him.... A heavy feeling hit the pit of his stomach at the thought. She was everything to him. His rock and his lover and his best friend and his sanity in an insane world. He knew when he drove in the driveway that she'd be waiting, ready to talk, to laugh or just to sit and watch the sunset. She didn't want to talk shop or listen to the latest gossip that Hollywood seemed to feed on. She didn't even want to discuss her own cases that much. And still they found plenty to talk about. The world, the weather, the nebulous state of careers were all topics of conversation. It was mind cleansing to be with her. Yet he couldn't really explain the chemistry that existed between them. He could give all kinds of reasons, but none was really comprehensive to anyone but him. She was his vitamin pill and tranquilizer all rolled into one.

In four weeks he'd be proposing marriage. He rolled the thought around in his mind and it still brought untold pleasure.

As he swung the car into the driveway he was smiling.

APRIL STOOD IN THE KITCHEN, her dress covered with the frilly apron, her high heels and makeup on, stirring the scallops and scallions in the pan. Her head was bent as she frowned at the slip of paper that held the instructions for the meal. Somehow, when cooking this recipe the last time, she had dropped a dollop of cream over a crucial portion of the instructions. Was it a half tablespoon of anisette or a half cup? She couldn't tell and her memory had deserted her. Somehow a cup seemed too much, but the tablespoon looked as though it were too little to matter. She shrugged. Somewhere in between seemed okay to her. She'd just play it by ear; after all, anisette couldn't harm the taste too much as long as she was careful. Having made the dinner once before and it having turned out right gave April a boost of confidence.

When the front door rattled April ignored it. Jace had his key, she was sure. Then she remembered her role and raced out of the kitchen, ready to greet him with a smile and a frilly apron showing her domesticity. She ran toward the door at a dead run, almost tripping in her high heels. Jace's eyes widened as he watched her career into him. His arms automatically opened to catch her before she brought both of them to their knees.

"Hi," she greeted him huskily. He tried not to show his surprise at her attire. She put her hands on his shoulders so she could reach up and plant a wifely kiss on the corner of his mouth.

"Hi, yourself," he growled as he turned his head and gave her the kind of kiss he needed. A lover's kiss. He needed her touch after the day he had had. He needed her.

Her arms crept up farther, entwining his neck, and she kissed him back with all her heart, forgetting wifely-duty kisses in favor of touching and being with the man she loved. He sighed in her parted mouth, and she knew he had wanted an excuse to touch as much as she had.

Finally he leaned back and took a look at her, smiling with his eyes as he took in her clothing. "You're all dressed up. Are we going out?"

"No, we're eating in tonight. I'm cooking and you're praising."

"Good enough," he said with a sigh, slumping against the closed door, still holding her waist in the span of his hands. "I wanted a quiet night."

She smiled and touched his brow, then allowed her fingertips to soothe his temple, loving the texture of his skin. He looked so tired. "I'll get you a glass of wine," she said, taking his hand and leading him into the kitchen just in time to see a dark puff of smoke coming from the frying pan. "Oh, my God, my dinner!" she wailed, pulling off the pan from the burner. She peered past the smoke to the bottom, seeing small dark spots that resembled what used to be scallions.

Jace peered over her shoulder and sniffed. "Why don't you start again? It smells fairly salvageable."

"Starting again means that it isn't salvageable," she pointed out, becoming thoroughly depressed as she looked down at the burned food in disgust. Why couldn't he have been here when everything had gone so smoothly? Why did she have to goof up now? The answer was simple: Jace was here, taking away her concentration, as usual.

"Just a suggestion, honey," he murmured placatingly, having the good sense to know when to keep his mouth shut . . . this time.

April's dinner set the tone for the entire evening. Everything was either slightly undercooked or slightly overcooked. But the wine was chilled just right.

After dinner they sat in the living room and giggled through a situation comedy that a mutual friend was starring in. Then they raced breathlessly around the pool until April let Jace catch her.

It was almost eleven before they showered, soaping each other with an overabundance of lather. They dried each other off with care, then fastidiously wiped down the shower as the housekeeper had taught them to do to keep the water spots away.

They climbed into bed yawning. April rested her head on Jace's shoulder, burrowing her nose into his chest, as always. His hand gently wrapped about her hip, feeling the soft texture of it. They slowly began making love, bodies curled to each other; hands touching, gentling; only to fall asleep in the middle of a caress.

April's last thought was that Jace hadn't mentioned the clean house and the hours she had spent to get it that way. She smiled sleepily. It was just as well, for he also hadn't mentioned the fact that she had poured too much anisette over the scallops. You win a few, you lose a few. . . .

5

"WHY SHOULD I have to take her out? Find someone else to pander to her whims Friday night. After all, you've got two more days before the premiere. I have a private life, and it's one that doesn't include another woman, let alone an *actress!*" Jace barked at his agent. They were downtown in Sid's elaborately decorated office. Blowups of all the great stars—a few were Sid's other clients, but most of them not—adorned the walls, peeking out from behind the large, expensively fake plants.

Sid's hands patted the air, and his face showed the concern he felt at Jace's anger. "Calm down, Jace, it's not the end of the world. All the studio's asking is that you escort Sandra Tanner to the premiere of her last movie. When you signed to do this movie with her, you also willingly signed for publicity. That's why they paid you so much extra. You've been in the business long enough to know that. This is damn good publicity for the movie you're now shooting, and you know that, too."

"And I also know I don't want to date *that woman!* She already walks around with stars in her eyes and an imaginary wedding ring on her hand. Those eyes of hers look at me as if I'm real apple pie and she's an

American in Europe! Dammit, Sid! She *believes* this publicity garbage. This girl's living in a dream world! She's actually waiting for me to propose!"

"No, she's not," Sid said placatingly.

"Yes, she is!"

"Well, maybe," he conceded.

"Not only that, but she acts younger than some teenybopper! She doesn't have an opinion that's her own, let alone an original thought! She's boring!"

Sid sighed. He rolled his eyes back before he finally admitted the truth. "So what if she is? All you do is keep your mouth closed and everything will be fine. It's only for one evening, Jace. She can't very well marry you if you don't ask her."

Jace slammed his hand against the wall, then leaned his head on his arm as he took deep breaths in an attempt to control his temper. Finally, making an effort, he turned around. "Look, Sid, I'm trying to explain to you so you can explain to the studio. I already have a girl, and she's the one woman I want in my public and private life. In fact, she's the *only* woman. Period. I don't need this complication right now, and taking Sandra out will only complicate matters. They wouldn't have a blooming romance if I was married, so they can damn well do without it now. Do you understand?"

Sid nodded his gray head. "I understand, but you don't. When you signed this contract, you promised you would do whatever publicity necessary. You're not married so it's an academic question. So far you've turned down three major opportunities, and now they're insisting on this. You have no choice."

"What three opportunities?" Jace glared at the man. "Are you talking about flying to New York for that disco opening?"

Sid nodded. "That and the 'Today' show you turned down, along with taking photos with Erica in Mexico last week."

"You call that publicity?" he asked incredulously. Jace leaned over the desk toward the face of his agent, but the man would not back down. Nor would he be intimidated. He sat still, staring at Jace with sad gray eyes.

"You know it was. Now you don't have a choice. You have to do this, or you can kiss away the opportunity of making, or at least finding the backing for a few of those more dramatic movies you want to do so badly. Word travels pretty fast in this industry, and you'll be labeled 'difficult' in no time."

"There are other ways to get backing besides the studios. I could even start up my own production company." Jace stared hard at the older man, but the real answer was on his face. Finally all the fight slowly left his body, and he slumped into the leather chair.

"You win, Sid," Jace said, his voice dead.

His agent stood, a smile on his lined face. He patted Jace on the shoulder. "Don't worry, Jace. It'll all work out. I promise. I bet that if you explained it to her, April would understand, too," he said, attempting to soothe his star.

"Humph!"

"It was April who was with you at the party last week?"

"Yes." Jace stared down at the floor, his dark brows still etched together.

"I've only met her a few times, but I'd be blind not to notice how lovely she is. She also didn't seem to mind the photo session you and Sandra had to endure. Are you sure you're not making more out of this than there is?"

"Believe me, Sid. I'm sure."

Jace walked out of the office a little later, hands in his pockets, eyes on the plush carpet. He didn't want to see Sid's tittering secretary make eyes at him any more than he wanted to attend a premiere.

Dammit! If he had married Flynn earlier, he wouldn't be in this spot! Any publicity, no matter how distasteful, would be done with her at his side, instead of some empty-headed actress. But now, because he was single and had starred in so many romantic comedies lately, he had to do it or make things even stickier. At least he felt he had to if he really wanted to sink his teeth into a dramatic role. He'd be good in it, he knew. He was tired of light comedy, although it was the vehicle that gave him his start.

It was time for him to stretch his legs and try something different and challenging. If he could find the right dramatic script and the right supporting cast, he'd be good. Maybe even Oscar material. *Hold, it, Jace old boy. Don't count chickens. . . .*

But right now he had no choice. He either played ball in their court, or he'd have a hell of a time playing ball at all. It was as simple as that.

Now what would he tell April?

APRIL HAD GOT HOME EARLY and was relaxing with a law book she had been trying to read for the past six months. If anything made her want to do something else, such as get ready for dinner, it was this book. When the phone rang, April placed her finger in the text as a mark and answered. She had wanted a diversion, but she hadn't wanted client problems. Suddenly she hoped it was Jace.

"Hello?"

"Hello, who's this?" a young woman's voice demanded, and April had the feeling she had heard it before.

"This is the cleaning lady. Who's calling?" April snapped, in no mood for cute games with stuck-up starlets. Especially a starlet who hung on Jace as if he were the moon and she a not-too-bright cow.

"This is Sandra Tanner. I want to speak to Mr. Sullivan."

"He's not here right now," she replied in a sickening sweet voice. "May I help you?" Fly to the moon? Catch a slow boat to the North Sea? Drown?

"Just tell him to give me a call. We have a date for Friday night and I need to know what time he's picking me up," Sandra answered before the phone went dead.

So did April's pulse, only to begin beating again erratically. Nerveless fingers replaced the phone in its cradle. Sightless eyes stared at the wall, seeing instead the picture of Jace and Sandra as the cameras clicked and voices laughed. Had they been acting or was it real, that tension that had sizzled the air? When Sandra had made cow eyes at Jace, had he really been returning her feelings and April had only thought it was all an act? April's hands clenched as she remembered the soft words and small giggles and seething looks that had passed between Jace and Sandra.

She had been a fool! Jealousy filled her to overflowing, blocking out all reasoning ability. Her blood ran so fast all she saw was a burning red. Slowly, slowly, she took deep breaths, needing to calm herself before she could begin to move across the room. With precisionlike steps she aimed toward the couch, sat down and stared out at the patio beyond the glass doors. The anger slowly dissipated.

Then came the hurt. The law book dropped in her lap, and she looked down at it as if seeing it for the first time. An attorney. She was an attorney and she shouldn't be sitting here like this, hurting, just because some stuck-up starlet *thought* she had a date with Jace. Again her stomach clenched at the idea. She choked back the bile that threatened to rise.

All this time she had been working toward getting him to propose, while he was running around behind her back! No, he wasn't. She had to be fair. Sandra just said he was. That wasn't the same thing. That dirty, no-good bastard had used her as a stopping station when all the while he had other women on the side! No, he hadn't. Hadn't he spent all his free time with her? How did she know it was all his free time? Hadn't she just been taking his word for it? But she had to; after all, weren't trust and love the building blocks for their relationship?

She closed her eyes, willing the tears away that threatened to fall. She would ask Jace. She loved him and he loved her. He wouldn't do anything like this behind her back; she'd learned that much about him in their three years together. They had been together too long to go through this mental flogging. She'd trust and believe in him until she was otherwise proven wrong. And Sandra Tanner and her size D bra and Scarlett O'Hara waist could go chase cats, for all she cared!

She poured herself a glass of wine and sat down on the front patio to enjoy the sunset if it killed her. It wasn't long before she heard the sound of Jace's car as he drove up the last few feet of the road and into the driveway.

She turned her head and watched him as he approached. A casual black jacket was slung over one shoulder, his jeans were still creased and his black shirt was still unwrinkled. But his face was lined with fatigue. His brows were drawn down over his eyes and he wore a heavy frown.

April waved him to the decanter of wine. "Pour yourself a glass, Jace. You look beat."

His glance was quick but encompassing. It took in her tired and confused emotions quickly. His heart sank. "So do you. We make a hell of a pair today." He sat back in the chair next to her, wiggling as he got comfortable on the padded cushion before propping his feet up on the small adobe wall that ran around one section of the yard. "Something go wrong with a case?"

"No more than usual," she hedged, her eyes wary as she waited for him to say more. Her day had been blindingly good and invigorating, a direct opposite to her home life lately. When he leaned his head back and closed his eyes, she spoke again. "From the looks of your clothes, I'd say you'd been on the set and in wardrobe all day."

"You're almost right. I spent the last hour at Sid's office."

"Oh? Are you signing a new contract already?"

"No," he snapped, opening his eyes and staring down at the wine in his hand. He hesitated for a minute, then continued. "I was arguing."

Her heart began thumping erratically. Here it came. "About what?"

"About publicity and the many ways to achieve it."

"And. . . ?"

"And I lost." He stole a glance at her to see how this was going, but there was nothing on her face to show that she understood . . . or cared.

"What exactly did you lose?" she questioned quietly. She took a sip of her wine, suddenly wishing it was Scotch. Perhaps this was what made alcoholics—anything was better than hearing truth and losing love.

"The studio says I haven't been doing enough of the publicity I had promised to do when I signed the contract for this movie, so they've set me up with a 'premiere date.' " Still there was nothing to show that she understood. This was going to be harder than he realized!

"What's that?" She played with her wineglass, staring out at the beautiful sunset she wasn't registering.

"It's a command performance. I have to escort Sandra Tanner to the premiere of her last movie." He gritted his teeth, waiting for her voice to rise and accuse him.

"Oh? That almost sounds like fun. When is it?" She sipped on her drink again before putting the glass on the small table between them and closing her eyes. She prayed he didn't notice her hands shaking and focused on forcing them to relax.

"Friday," he muttered, now openly watching her face. Other than her pulse beating in her throat, there was no reaction. Could she care so little? He continued speaking. "I have to take her and let the press believe there's a romance between us. Then they'll give more publicity for the movie we're doing now."

"A little silly, wouldn't you say?"

"Of course." He stared at her hard, wondering why she wasn't angry. Something was wrong, but he couldn't put his finger on it. This wasn't the April Flynn he had known and lived with for three years. This was someone else. Against his will, he found himself explaining. "I haven't been willing to do any publicity in the past, so this time they're threatening me with no more money to back a film I want to do, if I don't help out with this movie."

"Have they offered you publicity in the past?" Her voice was less than interested, almost asking the question because it was expected rather than because she wanted to know.

"I turned down the offer. It meant traveling away from...from here and I didn't want to do that. One was on TV and then some interviews with my mother." His voice turned cold, disgusted.

"So instead of doing publicity with your mother, you chose to do it with Sandra. Is that right?" She couldn't keep the cold tone out of her words. It hurt. It hurt so much that only fear was keeping her in the seat. Fear of leaving and making a fool of herself.

"No, dammit! That's not right! They didn't give me

a choice... they just told me today that I had to do this... or else!"

"Well, I hope you have a good time. Premieres are usually fun, I hear." She cleared her voice and continued, plunging headlong into a lie that would save her pride. "Besides, it's funny, really, but I have a dinner date with an attorney Friday night. He's working on a case in conjunction with mine and asked that we meet."

Jace's eyes narrowed menacingly. "You've never done that before," he accused.

"I know. This just happened to work out that way. So now you can have a good time and so can I. Neither of us needs to feel guilty because the other is home without company."

"How nice for both of us," he said sarcastically. "And when did you propose to tell me about this little 'date' you had lined up? Friday night?"

"As soon as I found out, which was today," she answered, restraining herself from crossing her fingers.

"Well, isn't that cozy."

She opened her eyes and looked at him, surprise written on her face. "What's the matter, Jace?"

"Oh, nothing! I come home after a rotten day, only to find *my* lady has a date with another man!"

"It's only business. Isn't that the same thing you're doing? Isn't your date business, too?" she asked in an innocent tone. She reached down and grabbed her glass for something to do. His eyes were blazing heat in her direction, and she had all the heat she needed. A little Dutch courage wouldn't go amiss right now.

"Of course mine is business! I'm just not so sure yours is!"

"As much as yours is, Jace." She turned and looked him in the eye for the first time since they had begun this conversation. "Are you saying it's all right for you to date another woman, one who is crazy about you and lets the world know it, but that I shouldn't have dinner with a fellow attorney and exchange business information?"

He read her challenge correctly and knew he was beaten. For the second time in a day he felt the fight leave him. "No," he said in a low voice. "I'm not saying that. I'm saying I don't like the idea of your dating someone any more than I like the idea of my taking that empty-headed little starlet to a premiere where everyone will think I enjoy that type of woman." Frustration laced his face and anger his words. "But I'm forced into this date while you, you've chosen it! Dammit, Flynn, you have no right!"

"Did you tell Sid that?" she asked quietly.

"Yes! I did! But because we're not married, the world, not to mention the publicity department, doesn't recognize our commitment." He watched her blanch and knew he had touched on a subject they had both carefully stayed away from these past three years. He took a deep breath and then spoke more quietly. "But I thought you did, Flynn."

"I do. As much as you do," was her answer.

No more was said for the rest of the evening. They had soup and sandwiches for dinner, then read in the living room. Aside from an occasional, "Would you pass the salt," or "More iced tea?" no other questions were broached.

Thursday morning was no better. They shared a

cup of coffee in the bathroom as usual. Then they dressed and left in separate cars. By the time April got to the office she was a basket of nerves.

"How's the Great Plan coming?" Sam asked, placing a few new documents in front of her.

"Stalled, I think," she answered in a monotone voice. Then her eyes lit up and she stared at him, her mind working furiously before her mouth formed the words. "Sam, could you do me a big favor?"

A wariness invaded his eyes. "If I can and it's not against the laws of man and nature," he said.

"It's not," she replied, her voice filled with a determination he hadn't encountered before. "I need a date with an attorney. Good-looking—no *great*-looking—and willing to have a free dinner. Friday night."

"What for?" His eyes narrowed. He could see the wheels in her head turning at full speed, but he couldn't see where they were going.

"To discuss the business of law and be my companion for the evening, of course." She grinned in appreciation of his confusion and the simple answer to her solution. "It's all aboveboard and very easy. He just has to meet me outside the restaurant of my choice, dine with me, then leave. That's all."

"Won't I do?"

"No. Sorry, Sam, but it took two years for me to make Jace understand and accept our relationship. He was raised to believe that no relationship between two people of the opposite sex could really be platonic. I'm not jeopardizing that."

Sam shrugged. "If you don't think I wouldn't like a free meal and discussion of law, okay . . . ."

"That's not what I mean at all, Sam!" April finally realized her explanation was not quite adequate. "I'm looking for someone to make Jace sit up and take notice, not knock down and kick in the dirt! And you know how he'd react, I hope, to seeing us together."

Comprehension dawned. "Oh," Sam drawled, his dark-brown eyes finally widening in understanding. Then he grinned. Who said all men stick together? "In that case, I've got just the right guy. He's a Vietnam vet who's just now getting into law school. He's on such a tight budget and always starving. He'd love it. I think he's got a bit of the ham in him, anyway. Will Jace be there?"

"No, he won't," April said thoughtfully. "He has a premiere to attend. But I think I can get him to drop me off."

"This is really war, huh?" Sam said knowingly.

"Yup, a war of the worst kind—of the sexes." Her face showed her determination to win.

"God help the wounded," Sam muttered as he left. When he reached the door, he turned and added, "And I hope it's not you, April. Jace has more experience than you give him credit for. He could outmaneuver you on the battlefield with very little effort."

"I hope so, Sam," she said, giggling. "I truly hope so. To the wounded goes the sympathy. Jace always has championed the underdog." The giggle left her voice as she finished putting her thoughts into words. Silently she gave a quick prayer. *As long as Sandra Tanner is not in the picture, I've got a chance at being the winner.*

Sam shook his head as he quietly closed the door and headed for the phone. He, too, said a quick prayer as he picked up the phone and dialed his friend's number. April was going to need all the help she could get. The funny thing was that he felt Jace would need it, too. April might be a woman, but she was *not* an ordinary woman! This was going to be one hell of a battle, no matter who won.

"CAN YOU PICK ME UP at work this afternoon?" April asked Jace sweetly on the telephone. "I know you have to leave early, but then so do I." She had waited until Friday morning before calling him at the studio. She wanted to make sure he couldn't find a way out of taking her home. "We both have to change for our dates, and...." She left the sentence dangling and could tell by the stiff silence on the other end of the phone he had filled in the rest of it.

"Four o'clock," he gritted. "Outside."

"That's perfect," she cooed before slamming down the receiver.

Step one was accomplished. Now for step two: getting him to drop her off at the restaurant where Leo was meeting her. She crossed her fingers and said another prayer. Lately she had prayed every day, but so far there had been no answer.

The ride home was quiet, the tension thick. Jace's knuckles were white on the steering wheel, while April's hands were knotted in her lap.

She wanted to turn to him, take him in her arms and plead with him not to go. *Stay with me and be my love* were the words that came to mind, but she knew she couldn't squeak them out of her parched throat.

They each dressed in silence, Jace on one side of the large bedroom, she on the other. Unshed tears kept blurring her sight, making it difficult for her to apply her makeup. Her ivory dress shimmered before her eyes. When she was finally through dressing, she waited in the living room, nervously pacing the floor until Jace joined her.

His manner was as stiff and formal as his perfectly tailored tuxedo. His tobacco-brown eyes were cold when he barely glanced in her direction. He went straight toward the bar and poured himself a Scotch.

"Is this 'attorney' picking you up?"

"No, I told him I'd meet him at the restaurant," she said softly, her heart dropping to her toes. He was angry but he didn't seem jealous, while jealousy was eating her alive from the inside. Any minute she expected to see big gaping holes in her flesh as a little green monster bit away at her. "I'm calling a taxi shortly."

"Where are you going?"

"Tracer's Lodge, a new place down on the strip."

He nodded, his frown darkening. "How are you getting home?"

"Leo will drive me to my car."

He gulped down the golden liquid, then filled his glass again. He turned to stare at her, and she grew even more uncomfortable and nervous under his gaze. "The studio is sending a limousine any minute. We can drop you off." His glass was once more raised and emptied. The glass came down on the bar top with a crash.

She jumped. He ignored her. They waited in stilted silence for the limousine to arrive. It was the longest, most trying fifteen minutes April had ever experienced. Just as she was about to break the silence and confess all, throwing herself on his mercy, the doorbell rang. With mingled feelings they walked out the door, Jace holding her elbow tightly as he guided her to the car. His grasp was painful and suddenly her anger was up again. How dared he be mad at her when he was the one who couldn't say no!

But as the chauffeur opened the rear door of the limousine, April realized the worst was yet to come.

Sandra Tanner, practically lying on the plush dark-gray seat, her eyes somnolent with restrained passion and her mouth pouting in its need to be kissed, was there in all her ungirdled splendor. Her gown was in the forties style, gold lamé and skintight with a brooch barely holding two pieces of fabric together on one slim white shoulder.

April looked at Jace, her eyes darting blue arrows of anger while his face showed the shock of seeing her. So much for this being planned...at least on Jace's side, she thought with satisfaction.

"Hello, Miss Tanner. How are you this evening?" April said brightly, ignoring the hand that wanted to squeeze her elbow off. "Jace has offered me a ride. I hope you don't mind."

"'A ride'?" Sandra tried to sit up, but apparently her reason for lounging was that the gown was too tight to sit upright in comfortably. She leaned back once again, but her decorum had been shattered.

"Yes, I have a date close to where you're going, so

Jace kindly offered to drop me off," April said as she pulled down the padded stool in the center and opposite the back seat and smoothed her crepe dress over her knees, daintily crossing her ankles to give Jace a better view of her legs. A frown creased her brow and she looked at Sandra worriedly. "I didn't realize you would be picked up first, so I accepted his offer. You don't mind, do you?"

"She doesn't mind, Flynn. Now be quiet," Jace gritted between closed teeth as he sat down next to Sandra. But a wide expanse of seat was between them, and April stared at it with a smile on her face. This acting thing was easier than it was cracked up to be!

Sandra glanced from Jace to April, then back again. "Do you, do you two...?" She obviously hadn't known about their relationship. April smiled again. This poor girl was hot on the trail of a macho movie star and she hadn't bothered to check out his private life!

"Are we married?" April said quietly but with a smile. She didn't dare look at Jace, but his scowl could be felt in the space between them. "No. Jace doesn't believe in that sort of thing." She hesitated. "We just live together. We have for a long time."

A grenade couldn't have been more shattering in the close confines of the car.

"Flynn." Jace warned, but when April looked at him, she saw the small but definite gleam of mischief in his brown sexy eyes.

She laughed lightly. "Oh, it's okay, Jace. I bet Sandra is a thoroughly modern woman. She's heard of people living together before."

Harlequin Temptation™

Have you ever thought
you were in love
with one man...only
to feel attracted to another?

Sandra quickly captured and held on to what was left of her composure. "Not a unique arrangement. How long have you two been together?"

"Long enough," April said, only to hear Jace utter the exact words at the same time. They looked at each other and burst into laughter. How many times in the past three years had they done that before? So very many, which had always proved to both of them that even their thinking was on the same wavelength.

Suddenly April's smile dissolved. She had meant that it was long enough for them to be married by now. But what had Jace meant? Had he meant the same thing, or did he think they should be parting? She searched his face for the answer but it wasn't there. His head was turned and he was staring out the window as the limousine turned out of the drive and edged down the first hill.

"Then why . . .?" Sandra's face was the picture of confusion. April almost felt sorry for her.

Jace glanced back at both women. Suddenly his expression relaxed. His voice was soft as he completed the question. "Then why the date tonight?"

Sandra nodded, ignoring April altogether now.

"Publicity didn't tell you?" Jace asked quietly, and April almost felt a stab of pity for the young girl. Almost. When Sandra shook her head, he answered, "I'll explain it later."

With the exception of Jace's telling the chauffeur where to drop off April, the drive was quiet the rest of the way to the restaurant.

April's spirits continued to plummet with each mile the car ate up. This was no longer a game or a lesson for Jace to realize how much he loved her. This was cruel and indecent treatment of one human being by another, and all three were hurt by this evening's charades. Suddenly she wished she had voiced her fears and hurts and taken whatever had been Jace's verdict about their relationship. Her skirting the problem by adding another was probably the worst thing she could have done. She had acted the coward by not airing everything with Jace. Two wrongs did not make this fiasco right, no matter how she justified it.

And now it was too late to say anything. Or was it? She looked at Jace, taking in his profile as he stared out the car window. Leaning forward, she placed her hand on his knee to gain his attention.

"Jace," she began, only to have him pull his leg out of her reach. The car stopped, and she followed the line of his frozen gaze.

Leo stood on the curb, obviously waiting for her. He was better looking than even his picture had proclaimed him to be. About the same height as Jace, with the same broad shoulders, he was well built and handsome. His hair was blond, his brows dark and his eyes, peering at her intently before he smiled, were hazel green. A perfect specimen that she wished she had not called upon to solve her problems.

She glanced back at Jace, fleetingly noticing the actress's interest glowing in her eyes. Jace sat rigid in his seat, his eyes sparking contempt at April. He was furious. There was no other word for it.

With more control than she had ever seen him use before, he carefully opened the door and turned to help her step out. His hand was cool and impersonal; his eyes wouldn't even connect with hers.

Leo came forward. Putting his hands on both her shoulders, he murmured her name and kissed her soundly on the cheek. His eyes were lit with merriment; apparently he had been properly primed by Sam. "I thought you'd never arrive," he said in a low, gravelly voice.

"But I'm here," she answered inanely, not sure what to do next.

She needn't have worried. Within seconds Jace was back in the car and it was pulling down the street, speeding as it entered the mainstream of traffic. She watched it disappear, tears once more welling in her eyes and her heart almost breaking with the sadness of their plight. The back of Jace's head was leaning perilously close to the beautiful blond actress with him.

6

APRIL'S APPETITE WAS NIL, but the meeting with Jace outside the restaurant hadn't seemed to bother Leo at all. He had charmingly smiled her off the sidewalk and into the restaurant, gallantly taking over the ordering of food and wine as if he had planned the date and not she.

His eyes twinkled and his chuckle was dark and deep, reminding her of Jace all over again. And soon he had her relaxing. In fact, with his running monologue of interesting events in his life, he had her smiling by the time their main course was served. The guilt of realizing what she had done to her relationship with Jace still lingered in her eyes, but no one could meet Leo and not like and respond to his personal brand of nonsense. He was like a giant, tan-and-gold teddy bear: darling to look at but even better to cuddle—or in this case, listen to.

Leo looked at her plate, then winked at her. "I thought all your money was going for naught when you picked at the appetizers and then played with the salad. I can see, though, that I just didn't order the right things. A broiled redfish seems to suit you."

April chuckled. She had only eaten three bites, but it was better than anything else that had been placed

in front of her. It tasted like sautéed sawdust, instead
of just the plain variety. "It's very good," she com-
mented, putting another small bite into her mouth,
pretending to savor the flavor.

"Is it good enough to enjoy, or just good enough to
fend off hunger?" he asked, and at her surprised look,
continued. "I have a vested interest in your appetite.
After all, if you go home and fix a bologna sandwich
before going to bed, then certainly someone would
know you had lost your appetite at mealtime. It would
be a dead giveaway." His eyes twinkled. "'Someone'
might even get the idea you enjoyed my company so
much you weren't hungry until you were away from
me."

April leaned back, seriously looking for the first
time at the bright and capable man seated across from
her. He was handsome to behold and marvelous to
converse with. He had strong features and a striking
build most women would love. But he wasn't Jace Sullivan, and nothing could negate that fact.

She placed her fork on her plate, giving up all pre-
tense of eating. "Why did you do this, Leo?" she
asked, curiosity getting the best of her. "Why would
you want to go out with a perfect stranger and have
dinner, not really knowing what you were getting
yourself into."

"Because Sam asked me to," he said simply. "He
said you were a good lawyer in need of a friend. I took
Sam's word for the rest. Since he's helped me by tutor-
ing me through several tests, I owe him one. Besides, a
man with my big build and extremely limited finances
doesn't usually get a chance to go out with someone

like you and afford it." He grinned, and April grinned back. "When I asked Sam why he didn't take you out, instead, he told me he knew the enemy too well and the enemy wouldn't take Sam on in combat." His green eyes twinkled as he continued. "However, if the enemy was the man in the car, I'd say he'd have taken on Quasimodo if he thought you were interested in him.

April smiled, but the humor didn't quite reach her deep blue eyes. "Apparently not. He didn't take you on, did he?"

"Almost, Miss Flynn. Almost. I'd say that I hadn't seen control like his since my old army days. I'd also say that that control was as close to snapping as I've ever seen. That was one angry man."

Leo took a sip of his wine, then continued to eat his dinner, a huge rare steak, April couldn't remember the cut. He also had a plate of fried potatoes and two vegetables, along with a small loaf of hot bread. His dinner didn't look any better to her than her own did. But he apparently enjoyed it, steadily demolishing it bite by bite.

April finally pushed her plate away. Unable to get food past her closed throat was definitely a barrier to eating.

"Why don't you just tell the man you love him and want to marry him? It would certainly put him out of the misery I saw in his eyes tonight." Leo's voice broke into her thoughts.

She didn't know why she sat with a man she hardly knew and confided her personal secrets; she'd never done it before. Still, she did. "I've already told him the first part. My pride won't say the word 'marry.' He's got to want our marriage, or it would never work," she said, her voice low and dangerously close to breaking. "He's got to say it."

"I think he's already claimed you as his. The rest is just a formality." Leo finally put down his fork and knife and sat back, giving a satisfied sigh before smiling at her. "Maybe you have to do a little plea bargaining with him."

"Jace? Plea bargain?" April laughed, but it almost sounded like a choke.

"Sure. If he wants you, he has to marry you. It's as simple as that."

"And if he says no?"

"Then he's not worth it," Leo said with conviction. His green eyes suddenly twinkled like a leprechaun's. "But I'd bet my next semester's tuition that he'd jump at the chance to keep you."

Hadn't Sam said just about the same thing to her when she'd started this whole thing? "Really, I—"

"I don't bet things like tuition lightly," he pointed out, staring directly at her. "You're a looker, Miss Flynn. And in a tinsel town of fakes, you're real." The intensity of his eyes and the way he leaned forward told April he was sincere. He was also flirting, and she didn't need any more casualties in her life.

"Thank you," she said quietly, and made an effort to keep the conversational ball in a more impersonal court.

The rest of the evening was devoted to discussing his work at law school and her practice, making April feel more secure in his company, if not happy.

He drove her back to her car around eleven that evening, but as she began unlocking her door, she glanced up to realize there were lights on in her office. Making her decision quickly, she pulled out her keys and headed for the building.

When she opened the office door she saw Sam sitting at his desk, reading as he took notes from one of her law books.

She gave a strained grin. "Studying this late? It's nice to see a student so hard at work. I'll have to have a talk with your professor to let him know just how dedicated you are."

His startled look turned into a weary smile. "Don't overdo it. I have a big exam Monday. Otherwise I'd be with a lovely lady, having dinner and figuring out how to make my next move." He leaned back, throwing his pencil down. The chair creaked against his weight, but he didn't seem to notice. "How was Leo?"

"Perfect." April threw her keys in her purse and sat in one of the uncomfortable reception chairs. "We had a nice dinner and he dropped me off here. I was about to leave when I saw the light in the window, decided to investigate, and here I am."

"All in one piece," he added dryly, placing his hands behind his head and stretching. "What about Jace?"

"Jace continued on his merry way with Miss Starlet. End of story."

"How did he react to seeing Leo?" Sam prodded, wanting to know the details.

"Angry. Leo thought he was jealous, but I know

better. I've seen that look in his eyes before, and it was only there when somebody crossed him. Other than that the dinner was fine."

"Jace has never had reason to be jealous before, so it might be that you've not had enough experience with 'that look,' as you call it."

"Oh, I know," she answered wryly. "At that moment I could have been any one of a number of possessions that he had misplaced. It was the same look."

Sam shifted his seat. "When is he due home?"

April gave him a bright look, trying hard to keep the conversation light and airy. "Jace didn't say. He keeps his dates and his check-in and check-out times to himself."

Sam muttered an expletive under his breath as he brought the chair down on all four legs. "April, why the hell don't you tell him what you want, instead of playing games. It's not like you. You're not very good at it, and he doesn't expect it from you...."

April stiffened. "I'm not playing games. I'm trying to make Jace see the light. If I don't succeed in the next three weeks, then we're finished." Just half an hour ago she had been ready to take him on his terms. Now she had swung back to her original idea. Oh, well, it was the prerogative of a lady to change her mind, especially when the lady was getting ready to explode with frustration! She tried to smile at Sam to show how little she cared, but knew it looked more like a grimace.

"I don't believe you!" he exclaimed, his confusion clearly written on his face. "You two are in love! Why on earth would marriage be so important!"

"Because I need his public commitment," April said softly but with all the conviction in the world, showing Sam better than any words just how traditional she was. "I need to know that Jace is mine, that he wants to tell the world I'm his. It's old-fashioned, but I need it."

His voice was filled with concern. "Are you sure, April? Is that really what you need?"

She nodded, tears beginning to trickle down her cheeks. "I want a house that's half mine. I want children in the yard who squabble and laugh and look like Jace. I want his love for me alone. And I want his name. . . . Don't you see, Sam? I need him."

Sam came around from the desk and stood in front of her. She looked so very bruised and tired and in need of a friend. He'd always seen her so confident that this side of her confused him. He wasn't sure what to do. "Come on," he said softly, holding out his arms to her. "What you need is a good cry."

And cry she did. She stepped into his arms and used his shirt for a handkerchief as she cried the events of the night away. But most of all she cried for her bad lack of judgment in doing what she had done tonight. It wasn't like her to play at being sneaky, especially with Jace. And now that she had, nothing had changed except her own opinion of herself.

By the time she was finished, her face was blotchy and her eyes swollen. She sniffed. Her nose kept running and neither of them had a tissue. Finally she hiccuped her predicament and made her way to the washroom.

She rinsed her face in icy water, removing what remained of her makeup at the same time. It had taken her almost an hour to apply that makeup and less than fifteen minutes to cry it off. She stared in the mirror. Her beautiful ivory dress had damp splotches on it that seemed to meld with the creases. She looked old and tired and all used up. Tiny lines were fanning out from the corners of her eyes. She realized they were there because of laughing, but they would also deepen from this time on. She was getting older and no wiser. Would Jace be the kind of man who'd enjoy living with an older woman? Or would he want someone younger, prettier, sexier? Would he tire of her because he knew her so well and there was no challenge left? She looked again, her sad blue eyes staring back at her in commiseration. And what about herself? She knew she loved and wanted Jace. But was she a career woman who wanted children and a husband and a quiet life, or did she want only the excitement of the court, new cases, new trials? Perhaps both? She knew the answer: both. Neither one would taste as sweet without the other. . . .

JACE DROVE LIKE A MANIAC down the canyon road, his hands clenching the steering wheel and feet slamming the pedals as he veered around the sharp curves. Damn April Flynn! He had already spent the most boring time of his life without her, only to go home and find she hadn't returned yet! Where on earth could she be? The answers that unwillingly popped into his mind made him speed down the road all the faster.

Everything had gone wrong. His mood. Sandra's

blatant attempts to seduce him and make intimate friends with the press. Sid's stern looks across the restaurant, telling him he wasn't acting enough of the perfect lover. His own thoughts of April in the arms of that, that, caveman hadn't helped a bit, either. Tonight had been the worst night he could remember in a long time.

He had sat stiffly through the premiere, Sandra's arm entwined with his as she smiled beguilingly at every reporter that passed by. She looked as if she had just received the Oscar—and he was it. At least the movie was cute and witty, a well-done piece of acting, directing and editing. At least he had enjoyed that. Until Sandra had leaned over, whispering bits of the plot just one minute before each section unfolded. It took away not only the anticipation but made it impossible for Jace to lose himself in the film. Besides that, she giggled in his ear, a high-pitched sound that set his teeth on edge and grated down his backbone. He finally decided that someone in high school must have told her it was a really sexy thing to do, because she did it constantly.

After the premiere they were shoved into a limousine and taken to a champagne party at one of the more prestigious restaurants on the Strip. It was closed to everyone except those invited to the opening. Jace was quickly bored, for it wasn't as entertaining as the movie had been. In fact, he hadn't even wanted to attend, but the look in Sid's eyes from across the theater lobby told him he had no choice.

So while Sandra giggled a story to reporters about a love scene she and Jace had just finished in their new movie, Jace had stood around with a stupid glass of champagne dangling from his fingers, wishing it were Scotch. By the time he knew he could leave, he was even wishing it were one of Sam's margaritas—anything as long as it was strong!

His head was filled with make-believe scenes of Flynn in that caveman attorney's arms: April kissing that caveman. April sighing in wonder from that caveman's expert loving techniques. April's soft skin and warm voice echoed in his hands and head, and he had to close his eyes to the vision he had concocted. He wasn't sure whom he wanted to kill first: April Flynn or the caveman. Against his wishes his body reacted to the thought of tenderly making love to April until she cried with ecstasy. He tried to erase the image of her from his mind with another gulp of champagne, but no matter what else he thought, the thought always circled back to remind him of making love to April.

When Sandra finally danced back to his side, the cameras were clicking again. She had obviously decided to play her little romance role to the hilt. She threw her arms around his neck and kissed him as if she had been gone forever. His hands involuntarily reached to steady her, accidently skimming over her breasts to circle her upper back. Her eyes widened as she threw her head back to stare at him, a slow smile gracing her face.

"I didn't know," she murmured seductively, rubbing her hips against him.

"I've got an idea you know even less than I ever gave you credit for," he snapped, not realizing how it would sound to her until after he said it.

"No," she said, giggling, pulling him closer so she could giggle directly into his ear and scrape his nerves raw with the sound. "But I can't wait to learn what you can teach. Perhaps later tonight?"

"That does it!" he growled, and pulled her arms down to turn her around and smilingly march her out the door. Enough was enough, and if Sid didn't think he had played his part well enough, then that was too bad!

Without compunction, he had the limousine driver drop Sandra off at her door, not even bothering to get out of the car, then gave him instructions to hurry to his home. He leaned back in the seat and closed his eyes. He wanted April. He needed the sweetness of April's kiss to wipe away the dirty feeling of bad business, April's gentle touch to take away the tension from his body, April's soothing voice to erase the high-pitched giggle that rang jarringly in his ear.

But home was anticlimactic. He could see from the driveway the house was dark. He knew without checking the garage her car wasn't there. Amazed at the disappointment that flooded him, he allowed the next emotion total freedom. She was still out with that blasted caveman!

He didn't bother reasoning out his anger. He didn't even attempt to see her side. All he could understand was that he needed her and she wasn't there! He jerked off his coat and jumped out of the limousine before it had even come to a full stop. His fury got him into his car and down the road, but he wasn't quite sure where he was really going. Where would he look for her? At the restaurant? No. They would have finished eating long ago. The caveman's apartment? He didn't know where he lived; he couldn't even remember his name so he could call him. Then he remembered her car. She'd have to go back to the office. He'd wait there. Then he'd kill the bastard, make love to her and think about killing her, too.

The first thing he noticed was that her Cadillac was in the parking lot. That meant she was still with the caveman. But where? He glanced down at his watch. It was eleven at night! His anger grew even greater. The second thing he noticed was that her office lights were on. His heart beat faster in anger and now it was practically climbing out of his chest.

So! She'd had the nerve to invite him up to the office for a nightcap. That was *his* territory! They were probably making love on the very same couch he had seduced her on so many times before! Those, those . . . names he had never voiced before flitted through his red-tinged mind. He'd catch those two-timers in the act.

Jace jogged across the parking lot and took the stairs two at a time. Reaching her third-floor office, he stopped at the door, listening as he tried to catch his breath. At first all he could hear was his own heavy breathing. Then he heard the muted murmur of Flynn's voice, then another man's. Her voice was soft, low-pitched. Sexy sounding. It must be the caveman with her.

His fists clenched at his sides. He took a few deep breaths to calm himself, but nothing seemed to erase the red lights from in front of his eyes. He was being torn in two with jealousy, and the pain was nearly

unbearable. He wanted to slap someone, hit someone, kill someone. He wanted to crush her to him and
make sure she remembered the imprint of him for all
time and know that she was his. He wanted to cry
out his anguish. But most of all he wanted a fight.

He listened again and there was nothing to hear.
Silence. Total silence. He took another deep breath.
He'd kill them. As he quietly opened the door, his
eyes darted around the room only to land on Sam's
figure, bent over the desk, jotting down notes from a
book.

"You!"

Sam looked up. Shock registered on his face before
his grin widened. It was turning out to be a busy
night. "Yes, me. Who were you expecting? A bogey-
man?"

He ignored the quip. "Where's Flynn?"

Jace was a walking bundle of anger and Sam knew
better than to interfere, but remembering April's
tears, he couldn't resist a little playing with the tiger's
tail. "Why? I thought you had a date with a starlet
tonight?" He glanced around Jace's stiff hulk, as if
checking to see if she was there.

Jace's expression turned even more thunderous.
"Don't push me, Sam. Where is she?"

"In there." Sam nodded toward April's office.

"With *him*?"

"No."

"Alone?"

Sam nodded. "Alone."

April turned off the water and heard muffled
voices. Her back stiffened at the sounds. Was Sam

trying to call Jace on the phone? Damn! Hadn't she done enough damage to their relationship already; couldn't he stay out of it?

She'd have to cut the call off now, if there was any way. She could always hang up the phone on their conversation, then carefully explain to Sam to butt out. With determined steps she walked into the outer office, not stopping until her eyes alighted on Jace.

His tuxedo jacket had been discarded, his hair was mussed and a beard was already beginning to shadow his jaw. He looked wonderful! Until she gazed into his eyes and saw the hatred there. It was then that she noticed the smear of lipstick slanted across his mouth. Her throat almost closed, trapping the air in her lungs. A pain, so intense that it lit a fire in her stomach, flashed through her body. She began shaking. Crossing her arms in front of her, she stared back at him, reflecting the hate he had glared at her.

"What do you want?"

"My God! What happened to you!" Jace exclaimed disgustedly. "You look like you've been rolled in the back seat of a car!"

"So do you," she stated, feeling shakier than she cared to let him see. "And *you* didn't have the decency to wipe *her* lipstick from *your* mouth before walking in here!"

Dark brows rose, and brown eyes stayed locked with hers while he reached for a handkerchief, wiped his mouth and then stared down at the crimson evidence. A deep red crept up from his neck to fill his usually tanned face. "I know what you're thinking, but it wasn't like that," he muttered.

"Don't tell me any more lies, Mr. Wonderful. The evidence is in your hands!"

"Don't throw around too many accusations, Flynn. And don't try to hide the fact that someone's been having a good time with you! That damn caveman must have kissed you enough to take off all your makeup!" he growled in return, taking a menacing step toward her.

Neither paid attention to Sam's grunt as he tried to keep the smile off his face. Both of them were fit to be tied, and all over a kiss. He grinned again, wondering how Leo would like his new nickname, "caveman." He had a feeling he wouldn't.

April glared back at Jace, but when she saw the predatory gleam in his eye, she knew it was time to retreat gracefully. She took two quick steps sideways, behind the desk and next to Sam.

Sam's head swiveled between the two of them. His eyes showed his concern but also his interest in the recent developments. He was sure they both loved each other too much to do any harm, and the conversation was nothing if not stimulating. Suddenly he found himself saying prayers that he would never fall in love and not be in charge of his own emotions. If this was love, he'd never make it past the dating stage!

Jace took another step toward her, and this time even Sam got a little worried.

"Stay where you are!" April cried as she raised a hand at him, warding him off. "Whatever you've come to say, you can say it from where you are."

"I think everything's been said. I just wanted to see

that you were all right." He looked her up and down, a sneer on his lips. "But it seems that you've shown your true colors at last and I worried unnecessarily. You landed on your feet, just like the rest of your sex."

"What did you think I would do? Cry myself to sleep in *your* home because you decided you needed *entertainment* elsewhere? Please! Spare me your concern!" She shook with the explosive mixture of anger and heartbreak.

"And what did you think I'd do? Waste my time trying to be true to someone who doesn't know the meaning of the word? Well, lady, at least we both know where we stand. You can collect your things tomorrow." His brown eyes narrowed in disgust. "I don't want to see you ever again. Is that clear?"

Sam cleared his throat. "Hey, wait just a minute—"

"Shut up!" both Jace and April yelled at the same time, then turned again to confront each other, ignoring Sam once more.

"There's no way you're getting rid of me tomorrow. I'm going up there tonight and collecting my things," she said coolly. "You don't frighten me, Mr. Sullivan. You touch a hair on my head, and I'll sue you so fast your head will spin all the way down the canyon! Then see how quickly you get publicity!"

"I should have known better than to trust you." Jace's eyes glittered. "The night I found you conspiring with my mother should have tipped me off to your real personality."

"Oh, yes, the old mother-complex routine," April said grimly. "You've used her for an excuse ever since I met you. She's your excuse to treat people like doormats. She's your excuse never to marry again. She's even your excuse to remain a recluse! It's a lot easier to hate her than to come to terms with your youth and take some of the blame yourself, isn't it! You stubborn jackass! You're so damn stubborn you haven't even begun to read one of the best scripts that has come your way! I know it's what you want because I *read* it! And all because you don't want anything to do with her! Talk about childish!" Her voice went higher with every sentence. "What was your excuse to eavesdrop on our conversation? Her again? Eavesdroppers never hear good of themselves, didn't you know?"

"I do now," he said, equally grim. "And as far as I'm concerned, you both come from the same bolt of cloth."

"Good. Because you don't deserve me any more than you deserve your mother's love. You're too much a loner for either of us, handing us your ego problems rather than trying to change yourself," she cried, her voice piercing the air with anger and frustration. She took a breath and continued in a lower voice. "Now you can get out of here and leave me alone. If you don't mind, I'll be there in an hour or so to pack my bags. Then you won't have to worry about my darkening your door again. Ever." Despair centered in the pit of her stomach, bringing with it an ache that made her want to double over and cry again. But she ignored it as she watched the anger on his face turn to a kind of cold nothing. He had killed her love and he didn't regret it. Not one bit.

"Fair enough," he said stiffly, turning toward the

door. With his hand on the knob, he took one more look at her over his shoulder. "I hope you like that caveman as much as you think, but I'll bet that you'll be tired of him in no time."

"No bets," she murmured, suddenly feeling like a wrung-out towel. "Please, just go." April felt the tears choking her throat but knew she had to hold them in until he left. She wouldn't, couldn't give him the satisfaction of letting him see her cry!

The door slammed and April turned to the shelter of Sam's arms, burying her head in his chest and once more crying as if her heart were breaking—only this time it was.

It was almost one in the morning before April was calm enough to get into her car and drive, for the last time, up the canyon road. She would face Jace one more time, and then it would all be over.

Over. This whole fiasco had been her fault. She never should have tried to fight fire with fire. She certainly never should have lied to him, telling him she didn't want to see him again.

But, then, how had he got that lipstick? It hadn't flown through the air to land indiscriminately on his mouth! Could it have been an accident? She couldn't tell, but everything she previously knew about Jace screamed yes. And the fact that Jace had come after her meant he must have been worried and jealous. It hadn't dawned on her before when he was in her office because she had been too upset to think clearly.

Now what? How could she repair the damage they had done to their relationship? She would admit to her part in this mess, but he would have to shoulder some of the blame, too. After all, he was the one who'd accepted the date first. Did Jace still want her enough to try to patch things up?

She couldn't begin to guess his thoughts. Suddenly she felt as if she had been living with a stranger. The Jace she knew hadn't been in the office tonight confronting her. That was someone else, but not her Jace. He had been so *angry*! So very *distant*. For the first time since she had known him she had been frightened.

She always knew, somewhere deep inside, that Jace was a formidable enemy, but she had never before seen him at his worst. With her he had always been loving and caring. Oh, sometimes, just as most people, he'd snap and growl, but he had never tried to hurt her deliberately or to wound her with words and accusations.

But, then, she had never before behaved the way she had tonight, either. She had been just as much to blame as he had. A replay of the ugly things she had said ran through her mind. She was ashamed.

She turned into the driveway and stopped the car. Flicking off the ignition and lights, April sat a moment and contemplated her next step.

She had to tell him she loved him. Also, she had to explain her actions tonight and ask for his forgiveness. Then she had to be attentive and listen to his apologies. . . .

With a strong resolve and wobbly legs, April approached the house. It was dark in front, but if she knew Jace, he was on the back patio.

She knew she was right even before she walked

through the living room. Snores greeted her loudly as she stood at the sliding-glass doors.

Jace was sprawled out on one of the padded lounge chairs, his head dropping off to the side. Between his legs was what used to be a full bottle of the most expensive Scotch money could buy. Now it was more than half-empty. His hair was mussed by the night breeze, his cummerbund undone and his tie untied. His arms dangled over the sides of the lounge; his mouth was slightly open.

The love of her life.

She grinned. Whether she was leaving or not, she had to put him to bed before the angle of his neck broke his windpipe.

It took her almost an hour to maneuver him out of his clothes and into bed. His body was almost deadweight as she tried to carry him into the bedroom, only to have him collapse on the bed, fully clothed. Getting his tuxedo shirt and pants off took longer than she would have ever dreamed possible. He muttered and murmured the entire time, his hands reaching up to stop her, and landing indiscriminately on a breast or hip and giving a squeeze. Then he would grin and chuckle, undoubtedly thinking of something she couldn't see the humor in. But once tucked under the sheets and asleep, he looked like the little boy April yearned for. His hair was tousled, his mouth curved into a smile, his dimples apparent. Damn him!

Then it was another hour of pacing the perimeter of the pool, trying to decide what to do. His drunken boyishness had taken most of the steam out of her anger. By then it was too late to leave—past three o'clock.

Giving a quick call to Sam to assure him she was fine, she undressed hastily, took a quick shower and climbed into the single bed in the guest room.

She had wanted to cuddle close to Jace, to feel his nearness and hope that he needed hers, but she knew this was impossible. If his drunken but playful attitude was any indication, he would pay for his self-indulgence with one large hangover. No sense tempting fate by waking up next to a swollen, sore-headed bear in the morning.

7

APRIL HUMMED AS SHE MADE the coffee stronger than usual. The soft gurgling sound of the bubbling coffee blended with her slightly off-key sonata, creating a form of auditory Dutch courage to keep her from bolting out the door.

She wasn't the only one who probably felt bad this morning. Jace was going to need all the help he could get when he woke up and realized just how awful he felt. A little vitamin C wouldn't be amiss, either, she thought, reaching for the small dark bottle to set on the table and act as a reminder.

She glanced down at her chocolate-colored twill pants and matching, loose-weave sweater and hoped she looked as good as she thought. Her makeup was on, hair brushed and smile in place. After clasping her hands in a fervent prayer and taking a deep breath, she was ready to beard the lion in his den.

She poured a cup of coffee for Jace and a mug for her, grabbed the vitamin from the counter and walked quickly down the hall. His door was barely open, and she gave it a light kick with her booted foot.

Jace sat in bed, scowling at the painting on the wall. His hands were behind his head, showing off the cording of his muscular, tanned arms. His jaw was emphasized by the sexy darkening of a new growth of beard. The sheet was draped across his middle, its whiteness contrasting with his own bronzed skin, and she knew that if she lifted the sheet, she would see his all-over, even tan. Her heart gave a flip-flop. He might be feeling rotten, but did he have to look so good while doing so?

Suddenly she was frightened. How was she going to get through to him? His dark-brown eyes swung in her direction, locking with hers and allowing her to feel his arrogance, displeasure with her and, most of all, his contempt.

She stepped forward, a stupid, slowly drooping smile plastered on her face. "Good morning! I brought a cup of coffee for your head, uh, hangover, uh, for you." Damn! She sounded like a star-struck teenager!

"What are you doing here," he asked in a monotone, running a hand through his uncombed hair. "I thought we agreed to disagree."

She nodded, handing him his cup. When he didn't move, she placed it on the table beside the bed. "We did, but I wanted to talk to you first."

"So talk."

She turned to the closed patio doors and stared out at the pool, trying to get her thoughts in order. When she glanced back over her shoulder, Jace's eyes were closed, and for a minute April thought he had fallen asleep.

"Well?" he muttered, and she realized he had been waiting.

"The least you could do is look at me," she said

angrily, suddenly frustrated at her inability to choose the right words.

He opened his eyes and stared straight ahead. "I'm listening."

Then she faced him, clasped her hands in front of her and closed her eyes. "I'm sorry for what happened last night. I set up that dinner with Leo deliberately to make you jealous so you could feel just a twinge of what I was going through, thinking about you and Sandra Tanner."

She held her breath as she waited for his answer to her confession. There was a moment of silence before Jace spoke. "Quit playing Joan of Arc and open your eyes and look at me."

She did. He was in the same position, only now he was staring directly at her. His heavily matted chest went up and down with his breathing. She watched, mesmerized. She was afraid to look in his eyes for fear of seeing his derision at her statement.

"Look at me," he commanded softly, his voice coming to her through a fog. Reluctantly she glanced up.

There was no derision there. His eyes glowed softly with tenderness and care and—April couldn't believe it—just a little bit of sheepishness!

"You're a better man than I am, Flynn. I tried, but I couldn't find the courage to say I was sorry for yesterday, so I acted like an ass, instead," he said softly.

"Really?" she whispered, clenching her hands even tighter.

"Really. I love you very much, counselor, and I want you to stay with me. Only I let my temper get in the way, and then I didn't know how to get out of the mess I made. I need you, April. My life wouldn't be the same without you in it."

"Really?"

"Really. In fact, I had to pretend to be skunk drunk last night so I could play on your sympathies in the hope that you would stay until this morning, when we could work it out." His voice dropped lower. "I was hoping you would climb into bed with me and I'd be able to woo you over to my side."

"Really?" She was still smiling, when the words he had uttered sank in. The smile slowly disappeared and a smoldering anger took its place. "Oh, really!"

"Damn," Jace muttered, "I knew I shouldn't have said that." He held out his hands in supplication, but April moved before he could speak.

With a flying leap, she was on the bed, lying across his stomach holding down his hands. Her blue eyes sparked fire, searing him with their intensity. "You're right, you, you, you actor! How dared you put me through last night!" She wiggled into closer contact with his hips. "You're horrible! Awful! You're a bastard!" she cried, sounding deeply offended. But her impish, delightful smile didn't match the anger in her words.

He looked up at her. "Were you really jealous, Flynn?" he asked softly, as if he badly needed her reassurance.

She nodded, her face losing its smile. "Very."

"Oh, God. So was I," he said, his voice still soft, and she watched his firm full lips move. "I couldn't stand the thought of another man being with you, touching you the way I do."

"Neither could I." Her answer was simple and direct; her eyes told more of the story.

Jace gave a sigh. "And you'll stay?"

It took her a minute to answer, and his breath caught in his chest as he waited.

"Yes," she finally said. "For now."

He sighed again. Loosening one hand, he cupped her face, stroking the softness of her cheek with his thumb. "Only for now?" his husky voice teased.

"I couldn't stand to go through this again, Jace," she admitted somberly. "I have no weapons with which to fight back. And even if I did, I don't think I'd know how."

"You did admirably last night." His thumb moved from her cheek to caress her lips, outlining them again and again.

Her lips parted as his touch sent shock waves through her system while she lay on top of him, starving for his kiss and holding back in anticipation.

Jace was playing the same game. His mouth opened the same breadth as April's, and he watched in fascination as her tongue came out, barely touching the tip of his thumb before hiding again.

"I promise you, April. I'll never do that to you again. Never."

His kiss was sweetened with the sugar of his promise, and she answered back the only way she knew how, with all her heart and soul.

He took her hands and placed them in a circle around his neck; then, with her anchored thus, he allowed himself the freedom of skimming his palms along her sides and back, molding her to him like a warm patty of softened clay.

Her sweater crept up naturally, and before April could take a second breath, Jace had pulled away from her mouth and lifted up the sweater, taking it off her slim form.

"Mmm, I love the feel of you," he said huskily as his hands cupped her breasts. "You have just enough for me. Not too much and not too little." His fingers played with her breasts, making them fit into the contours of his hands.

"What? After Sandra Tanner, everyone else must be a disappointment," April teased breathlessly, but her eyes belied the joke, showing her vulnerability.

"Since I haven't touched the lady quite as intimately as this, I wouldn't know."

"But you have touched her?" April prodded.

"Flynn," he growled impatiently, warning her that she was treading on dangerous ground.

"Then you have," she said softly.

Their bodies became tense and still. Each realized that they had reached a crisis point. April stared into the brown depth of Jace's eyes, her own silently begging for the reassurance she would not form words to ask for.

His reluctance was apparent as he fought for pride of silence over explanation. Explanation won.

He gave a heavy sigh. "Only once. When the photographers were snapping photos last night, she flew at me and gave me a kiss for effect," he said, irritation lacing his voice that he would even denigrate himself to explain. "That's why you found the lipstick there. I never kissed her, Flynn, she kissed me. In public. For effect."

"And?" April prompted. Jace's hands tightened on her breasts.

"And in order not to be knocked off balance, I grabbed her, well, what I thought was her waist."

"Only it wasn't?"

"Hell, Flynn!" he finally exploded in frustration. "She's shorter than you! It would have been *your* waist, but they were her *breasts!*"

April tried hard to keep her face from showing the giggles his imagery had drummed up.

"And did she mind?"

"I didn't ask," he said impatiently. "I just dropped my hands and told her it was time to leave." He took another deep breath and stared back at her, his features showing his wariness. "What about you?"

"Not even a kiss," she said softly, and watched relief flood his eyes.

His hands loosened their hold to tease the tip of her nipples; his legs opened to enable hers to lie in the center. "How about a kiss now?"

"Mmm," she said consideringly, smiling. "I wouldn't mind, but I won't be compared," she said.

"There is no one to compare to you, Flynn. And if there were, they'd have to knock me over the head to get my attention. Because I'm not looking. I'm happy with what I've got. Very happy."

A sadness made her blue eyes turn an almost gray. "That's why I said 'for now,' Jace. You never know when you may tire of me, and then you'll be gone."

"That works both ways," he said huskily, but his hands tightened their grip on her, as if he could ward off that day by holding her close.

She didn't answer, just leaned down and parted his lips with hers for a kiss that gave him all her love.

They made love all morning long: slow and gentle and sweet and sad. It was like a nonverbal recommitment to each other. And yet the strings that April needed to feel secure were nowhere in sight. She was still in limbo as far as their relationship was concerned. It was wonderful and heartbreaking all at the same time.

"SAM, HAVE YOU EVER been in love?" April fiddled with the pencil on her desk, her brow creased in thought.

Sam was fixing one of his "famous" margaritas for them after one of their busier days. His head was down as he stirred the drinks. Turning toward her, he grinned. "Nope," he said cheerfully. "And from the looks of the battlefield you and Jace are on, I don't think I ever want to be."

"Not ever?" April raised her brows in disbelief.

"Well," he replied, handing her a drink and sprawling in the chair across from hers. "I can't say I wasn't ever in love. There was a time...but I shouldn't count my fifth-grade teacher, who was one terrific woman in her day."

Now it was April's turn to grin. "Is *was* the operative term?"

"Sadly, yes. When I went into sixth grade, she married and got real fat. Sort of went to pot." He shook his head at the wonder of it all, but the smile was still on his face.

April could see him as a sixth grader; with that twinkle in his big brown eyes and that mischievous grin, he must have been the teacher's pet. Come to think of it, she'd bet he hadn't changed much, except the teachers had been replaced by all single women.

"You don't have to sound so cheerful, Sam," she admonished, but was unable to keep the twinkle from her own eyes.

"At the time I was devastated. Then I went into the seventh grade and learned the facts of life. There I realized she hadn't turned fat, she was pregnant. She gave birth to a pair of healthy twins." He chuckled as he looked into his drink, this thoughts turned inward. "When I realized *how* she got pregnant, my estimation of her went way up. I thought that the 'act' she had to go through to have children must have been awful for a sweet, angelic woman like her and she must only have done 'it' in order to have children. She had made the ultimate sacrifice for the sake of having a child. In my adolescent eyes, she was a saint who almost had to endure the fires of hell."

By this time April could no longer hold back the giggles. Her laughter echoed through the room, slowly joined by Sam's more mellow chuckle.

"And when did you take her off your saint list?" she gasped.

"The next year," Sam said without hesitation. "That's when puberty hit and I discovered 'that act' was really on the opposite swing of the spectrum I had placed it on."

Her giggles were barely under control but she managed to say, "Precocious, weren't you?"

"Hell, yes. As time progressed and I grew up, I learned that women were like fine wines, to be savored and enjoyed to the fullest...and I'm an alcoholic." He grinned, but there was no laughter in his eyes. "But to get back to your original question, other than my teacher, no, I've never been in love."

April sobered, her face registering the vulnerability of his statement. "Do you believe in love, Sam?"

His dark-brown eyes suddenly showed a confusion April had never seen before. "Since I've seen you and Jace, love would be a hard thing to deny." His gaze left hers to travel to the window. With an almost absentmindedness he sipped his drink. "It just doesn't seem to be a commodity that's in the stars for me."

"It will come," she said softly.

He gave an inelegant grunt. "I doubt it, April. I've traveled around the world, kicking here and there, even did a stint in the marines. It took me this long even to discover my niche, and if I haven't found someone by now, at the ripe old age of thirty-three, I doubt that I will."

He suddenly grinned again, and April was amazed at how handsome he was. She had never really noticed his quiet good looks before because their friendship was so solid. But looking again, she saw what other women must see and understood how he could have the pick of women to spend his evenings with. Funny, how she had never noticed before. If she weren't so in love with Jace....

Sam continued slowly. "I think I'll just carry on

sampling the different varieties of wines and leave the private labels to others."

April leaned back and took a sip of her drink, strangely shaken to realize she had found something so special with Jace while others were still so alone. She was lucky, very lucky.

Sam leaned forward. "Hey, don't you feel sorry for me, Ms Attorney!" he chided gently, realizing where her thoughts were headed.

"I can't help it, Sam. I'm so happy I'd like everyone to feel the way I do."

"Don't wish that on me! You used to be a sane, stable individual before Jace came on the scene. Since then it's been nothing but peaks and valleys. Just look at what happened last Friday and how miserable you and Jace were. If that's what love is, I'll take my 'lonely' life-style over yours any day!"

April laughed again, relaxing in her chair. "At least I have fabulous highs to go with my depressing lows, Sam. Looking back, it seems as if I might have missed the world if I'd missed Jace."

Sam stood, taking both now-empty glasses back to the small portable bar in the corner. "In that case, you'd better get home. Didn't I overhear you say you were going to an old Charlie Chaplin movie tonight?"

"Oh, my God," April glanced at her watch, then stood quickly and pulled open her bottom drawer, where she kept her purse. She deliberately side-stepped her briefcase as she headed for the door. This was not the night to take work home. "Close the office for me, will you, Sam? I'll see you tomorrow."

"Will do. Have a good time," he called out as she rushed through the reception room.

The door slammed on his words, and he chuckled at her eagerness. He glanced around the office, making sure that everything was ready for tomorrow. Suddenly the room was overly silent.

It was time to leave. There was a sweet little brunette from the law library who was waiting for him at a certain restaurant. A grin split his face in anticipation. And if everything went well, he'd be busy all evening...and it wouldn't mean poring over law books for a change.

JACE WAS WAITING IMPATIENTLY at the door for her as she drove up to the house. He stood with hands on hips, watching her park the car. "Where have you been? I was getting worried about you."

"I had a drink with Sam before I left. It's been a pretty hectic day," she said as she slipped out from the front seat of the car.

"Did you forget our date tonight?" His scowl was fierce, but April knew his bark was worse than his bite.

"In a word, yes. Until Sam reminded me, I was ready to fall on the couch and take a nap."

"You forgot our plans?" he asked incredulously. "How could you do something like that?"

"I forgot the plans, darling. Not you. I was wishing you were there so I could cuddle up in your arms and go to sleep," she explained patiently, and watched as his face cleared and a smile blossomed.

"In that case, why don't we stay home and I'll do just that—hold you in my arms until you grow sleepy or romantic, whichever comes first."

"Jace! Behave yourself!" she exclaimed, but couldn't help the rush of warmth that came with his words. Perhaps that was why women were turned on by his screen image. He was sexy and charming, yet earthy and honest. And so damn good-looking! He was wearing a pair of brown knit shorts and a crisp white shirt with brown piping that displayed his strong legs and muscled chest and arms. He looked like a vanilla cone with a trickle of chocolate topping . . . so very delicious to the taste.

He saw the instant flare of desire in her eyes and was in front of her in two seconds. His hands circled her waist, his hips resting against hers as he leaned back and studied her expression. "How should I behave myself, Flynn? Do you want me to be nice or sweet or charming, or would you like it if I was really bad?" he asked huskily, feeling himself respond instantly to her nearness.

"I'd like you to be good and charming," she murmured, pressing her lips against the hollow of his throat and feeling a tickle of hair there. "Save the bad for later. Otherwise we'll never leave."

He chuckled and placed a hand on her waist, leading her to his car. "Come on, then, let's get going before we change our minds," he murmured, tucking her into the passenger seat.

Jace drove swiftly and competently along the canyon road, but when he finally came to the highway he raced the car as if he were in the Indianapolis 500. April tightened her seat belt, hoping against hope she would live to see tomorrow.

He glanced at her, his lips curling into a tender smile. "Too fast, honey?"

"Much too fast," she said through clenched teeth.

And he slowed down to the speed limit, sighing as if he hated going as slow as the turtle when he should have been playing the part of the hare.

"Poor Jace, the things you have to do for love," April commiserated with a smile.

"Just remember these small sacrifices, Flynn. I'll collect on them someday," he teased.

Their mood set the tone for the rest of the evening. The movie, an old silent Charlie Chaplin, was delightful, and they ate popcorn and laughed their way through it and a Mack Sennett comedy, which was just as funny.

Jace did his imitation of Charlie Chaplin down the sidewalk on the way back to the car and April doubled over in laughter. From the back his walk looked more like a pregnant mule!

With careful planning, they chose an all-night hamburger stand that specialized in jalapeño cheeseburgers and stuffed themselves until April thought she was ready to burst.

"Ah," Jace said, sighing as he leaned back in the red, plastic booth and rubbed his full stomach. "They're right when they say the way to a man's heart is through his stomach."

"They are?" April's mouth dropped. Jace had never been one to be picky about his food or go into ecstasy about certain menus.

"Yes. Once you fill a man's stomach, his mind can wander to other things. Things such as naps, which lead to thoughts of bed, which lead to thoughts of sharing that bed. . . . " He leered and April laughed, saluting his thoughts with a chocolate shake. "But what I'd really like right now is a cup of coffee."

"I'll get the coffee," she said as she stood, grinning. "And then you can get busy thinking about those . . . other things."

Jace reached for his wallet, but she raised her hand in the air. "Nope, this treat's on me. And don't thank me. I know I'm generous to a fault."

"I always said I'd find a rich woman," he murmured as he watched her turn to walk away, his eyes obviously not on her purse but where she would carry a wallet if she were a man.

Glancing over her shoulder, she chuckled. "Aren't you the smart one!"

April approached the counter, surprised as she looked around and realized just how many people were at a fast-food restaurant at this time on a Monday night. The tables were almost all filled with both teenagers and adults. She caught a glimpse of the clock. It was already after eleven.

She ordered the coffee quickly, paying with the change in her pocket. Adding the necessary cream, she stirred, a smile still lingering on her mouth.

As she turned back, she saw a large group of girls giggling in the curving corner booth as they stared and grinned in Jace's direction. If she was right, it would take about another minute for one of them to walk up and the ice would break for a procession of autographing to start. She'd better get him out of here quick, or they'd never be able to leave!

"Come on, Sam," April said loudly as she drew near the table. "You can drink this in the car."

His surprised look quickly turned to one of understanding. Sam's name was the code word they used
when one of them realized they were about to be
swamped with fans. It also told the fans they might
be mistaken, confusing them, if only for a few
minutes.

With quick grace Jace was out of the booth and
almost to the door before the girls decided to follow.
He and April ran toward the car, with April dropping the Styrofoam cup on the driveway. The engine
revved and the two waved gaily to the dozen or so
girls who had watched them drive off.

"That was close," Jace said as he clasped her hand
and gave a squeeze. "It looked like their numbers
multiplied from the time I stood up to the time we got
to the car."

"They did!" April laughed. "I think some of the
other customers followed just to see what the parade
was about. But you can bet your buttons the crowd
would have grown even more if you had stayed there
another minute. We wouldn't have got away until
midnight once the management got hold of you for
an autographed photo."

"How did you know they recognized me? I didn't
hear my name being called out or catch any glances
from the other customers."

"My antenna was up. I'm always on the lookout for
pretty women who give you the predatory eye. One of
those girls might have been sixteen chronologically,
but she had the eyes of a knowledgeable old lady."
April's voice was filled with disgust to disguise the
jealousy that lurked just behind her words.

"Mmm, I should have paid more attention. I was too busy watching my woman wiggle seductively up to the counter to see anyone else. I hardly ever notice another female when she's around. . . ."

"Why, what a lovely thing to say!" April's eyes glistened. "It looks as if I'll have to stick to your side like glue, just to remind you of that little fact."

"Just calling 'em like I see 'em, ma'am," Jace teased, trying his best to pull her closer to him without allowing the gear shift to do surgery on her stomach. "Damn car," he finally muttered in frustration. "Remind me the next time we go out to take your car."

"Yes, sir!" April saluted, grinning at his irritation. What pleased her more was seeing his obvious need to have her near. He still cared, deeply cared. She hadn't ruined the relationship by having that phony date with Leo. Suddenly her smile dropped away. And he hadn't ruined it by having that date with Sandra Tanner. Sam's words drifted back to her, reminding her just how lucky she was to have found Jace.

"What are you thinking, Flynn?" Jace asked as they turned on the canyon road. "You're so quiet."

"Something that Sam said today."

"Oh? Words of wisdom?" His voice was dry.

She ignored his tone. "Do you know, Sam has never been in love?"

"Some men have all the luck," Jace teased.

She ignored that. "Poor Sam."

"Why 'poor'? He doesn't seem to mind. In fact, he appears to play the role of the perfectly happy bachelor better than anyone I know."

April leaned up and teased a kiss on the side of

Jace's neck, just below his ear, feeling his skin prickle at her touch. "Because 'poor Sam' has never known just how wonderful it is to be loved and to love. Someday he'll be all alone and lonely, with no one around to keep him company...." She glanced at him through her lashes. Was he taking the hint?

Apparently not.

"I'll agree that it's a shame as long as he doesn't love or want to be loved by *my* woman." His voice was gruff with emotion as he turned and gave her a kiss on the tip of her nose, belying the intense feelings for the woman next to him that swamped him. She was everything he needed and wanted and loved.

April chuckled aloud at his possessiveness, while inwardly cringing at his inability to follow her thoughts. Perhaps with time he would catch on....

They fell into a companionable silence, both more than tired after a full day and full evening, too.

April watched his strong, firm fingers curl to shift the gears, suppressing her desire to cover his hand with her own. She loved him so much, and at times like now, without his arms around her to muddle her thoughts, she knew she loved him, loved him with all her heart.

Jace turned the corner into the drive and steadily climbed up the hill. April's head rested on his shoulder in gentle trust, and he loved the feel of her leaning on him. He gulped the lump in his throat. She had become something more than an addiction to him. April Flynn was everything he wanted in his personal life. She was so much fun and so loving—so very *right* for him!

Was she hinting that she wanted a more permanent relationship, or was she beginning to stray from him so that she could find someone to grow old with? He'd have to push his Romeo instincts even further than he thought in order to dislodge that notion from her mind. His breath quickened in fear. If they ever ended their relationship, he knew he'd be devastated.

A chill ran down his spine as he remembered the night he had seen April with that, that, caveman. He had gone totally berserk. He knew it and had been ashamed of himself by the time he was halfway home from his confrontation with April. He had known he was acting crazy when he stepped inside the office, but some small demon in him wouldn't let things rest.

Then, when he arrived home without her, he had broken into a cold sweat from his actions and her reactions. She had been justified with her anger. Where did he find the right to crucify her when he had been out with another woman? It didn't matter that Sandra Tanner had kissed him. April had a right to be angry. He had wanted to call her and tell her he was wrong, but he couldn't. That was why he had staged that drinking scene. He couldn't face her and tell her how sorry he was for all his accusations.

But she could say she was sorry. April had apologized and admitted her actions. She had been bigger, more forgiving than he had. Something deep down couldn't make him say the words that April had said. He wanted to—Lord knew he wanted to! But his pride got in the way. Now that he knew just how strong his feelings were, he'd make sure he would never let his temper and stubbornness get in the way of their happiness again. He would never allow his jealous feelings to separate them.

Like a child, he almost crossed his fingers, knowing that intentions didn't always coincide with actions.

"WHAT DO YOU THINK? A deep-pile ski jacket or several heavy sweaters and a Windbreaker?" April asked Jace as he lounged in the living room, skimming through a script.

He grinned as she posed in her new ski jacket, showing the dimples she loved so much. The jacket was bright orange, with white stripes on the back and sleeves, and made her skin glow like a peach in summer. Her dark hair glistened with highlights against the brilliant color. "I think either would be good, but I'd really like to see you running around bare," he said with a wink.

"Bare, what?" She chuckled. "Bear coat? Bear crazy? Or bear clothed?"

He dropped the script on the floor and held out his arms, which she tumbled into and cozied against. His lips touched the top of her head as he whispered, "Bare naked, and you know it!"

"Crude," she cried, giving him a kiss on his chest through the cashmere sweater he wore. It tickled her nose. "And the day before the Sabbath, too!"

"But very necessary for what I want to do to you."

"And what is that, pray tell?" Her eyes danced impishly.

"Rape and ravish your tender little body for at least three weeks."

"Is that all? What are you going to do for the last week?"

"Rest!" he growled, tickling her ribs as he turned her around to lean delightfully on him.

The phone rang, interrupting their play. "I'll get it," April said, reluctantly moving off Jace's body. "You finish your reading."

But when she answered the phone, she wished she hadn't.

"I need to speak to Jace," Sandra Tanner said in a dismissive manner.

"And whom shall I say is calling?" she asked sweetly. Two could play this cute little game.

"Sandra. He'll know me," she replied confidently.

April pulled out the antenna on the cordless phone and handed it to him, mouthing the name of the caller. His impatience and irritation was gratifying.

"Yes," he answered, reaching out and holding on to April's hand before pulling her down to sit beside him.

"Now just a minute," he interrupted only to be silent again. April watched his brows form a deep frown, and her heart began pounding. Whatever the conversation was about, it wasn't going Jace's way. Cursing intermittently, once or twice more he tried to interrupt and say something, only to be stalled again.

By the time he clicked off the phone and threw it on the cushion next to him, his face looked like an angry thundercloud.

April moved the phone and edged closer to him, waiting for the words of reassurance she knew weren't coming. It had been bad news, she could tell,

but her mind tossed aside all the catastrophies Sandra
could cause and found nothing worth his anger.

"Well?" she finally said, and he looked at her as if he
were surprised to see her there. He had obviously been
deep in thought.

He sighed, frowned, then ran a hand through his
dark hair. "Damn!" he muttered under his breath. Then
he looked at her, and his eyes grew tender. His hands
touched the sides of her neck as he drew her closer. A
smile slowly formed on his lips. "Marry me, April
Flynn. Marry me and take me away from all this."

April gulped, then gulped again. Schooling her features to look noncommittal as she did in the courtroom, she stared back. "Why?"

"Because we're right for each other."

"I know that. But why now?"

"Because if we don't marry now, then that little she
devil has got me over a barrel. She went to the studio
and complained and cried all over the publicity office's shoulder, and now I have to do more publicity
with her to fulfill my part of the contract."

"And if you were married it wouldn't be expected."
April's voice was calm, but her stomach was doing
somersaults.

Jace didn't notice. He was staring at the phone as if it
were a lethal weapon. "Right."

April stood, slowly discarding her new ski jacket as
she walked toward the front hallway.

"Wait!" Jace said. "Where are you going?"

"To take a swim," she said over her shoulder, unwilling to verbalize her own confused feelings right
then.

Without gathering her suit, she stripped on the patio, discarding her clothing on one of the chairs, and dove into the bracing water. Swimming long hard strokes immediately to work off her feelings of dejection, she allowed her mind to go blank. Her anger wasn't half as great as her disappointment in Jace.

For three years she had waited for a marriage proposal, and when it came, it was delivered because the man she loved didn't want to go out with another woman! Tears caught her unawares and she realized she was crying. She stopped swimming, breathing heavily as she trod water. Damn Jace! He had no right to make her feel this way! No right at all!

Jace leaned casually against the doorway. He watched her with narrowed, hooded eyes. Although his body gave the semblance of being casual, April knew better. The tension showed in the knotted muscles in his arms as he jammed his hands into tight jeans pockets. "Worn out yet?" he asked coolly.

"No."

"When are you going to answer my question?"

"I think you know the answer, Jace Sullivan! Go find someone else to bail you out of your 'problem.' Anyone would do the trick, it doesn't matter who!"

"That's not true and you know it," he answered, his voice coated with steel. "I asked you to marry me. I expect an answer."

April angrily splashed the water in his direction, darkening the path of stone that surrounded the pool and blotching it a deep brown.

"Then hear this! No, thank you, Mr. Sullivan," she

mocked sweetly, bowing her head before glaring back at him. "Although I deeply appreciate the offer, since I'm supposedly a poor, single woman living in sin and you're the big bad man who's responsible. But somehow, despite your kind offer, I feel it's not a good idea to marry because your mate-to-be needs a skirt shield to hid behind!"

"Flynn," he warned, straightening.

"I don't know. It just doesn't seem conducive to a happy marriage, does it?" Her anger was masked by an innocent look. "I mean, someday I may exchange my skirt for pants, and then where would you be? No doubt exposed."

Before he could answer, she turned her back on him and began swimming the length of the pool again, needing to work off the urge to grab him by the neck and drown him...slowly, painfully, tortuously.

Any minute she expected a splash, indicating that he'd joined her to tell her off, but the confrontation never came. Anticipation of a persisting verbal battle turned to ashes in her mouth as she continued to work off her frustration and anger.

All this time she had been working toward the goal of marriage, and when he finally proposed, it was because of another woman! Granted he hadn't wanted Sandra to chase him, but was that because he didn't like her or because he was afraid he might like her too much?

With that sobering thought all the fight left her. She dragged herself out of the pool and slowly picked up her carelessly dropped clothing from the ground.

Battling tears and tiredness, she walked into the plush blue-and-cream master bath and closed the door.

It wasn't until she turned around that she realized Jace was sitting on the commode seat, watching her every move with dark, narrowed eyes. His face showed the anger that he, too, felt, but it also showed something else she couldn't define.

It was on the tip of her tongue to apologize to him, but the emotional woman in her overcame the unemotional attorney. She had done her share of apologizing. The rest was up to him. She kept her silence, but her look dared him to speak first.

When he finally did, his voice echoed off the ceramic walls and resounded in her ears.

"Three years ago you said that marriage was what you were after, but I felt I couldn't afford it emotionally at the time. Now I'm asking for that same commitment from you, and you're turning me down. Why? Is there another man? Is that it?"

"Three years you thought you loved me, but you couldn't marry me. Now I've become an excuse, something handy to keep you away from the things you don't want to do." April shrugged, turning away so he wouldn't see the tears forming in her eyes. "You've changed your mind. Why can't I? Is there another woman?"

"Don't be ridiculous!" he snapped. "If there were, then I wouldn't be asking you to marry me, would I?"

"Maybe, maybe not." She flipped on the nozzle of the shower, testing the temperature of the water. It could have been freezing cold and she wouldn't have noticed.

"Answer me!" He stood menacingly. "Is there another man? Is that it?"

"*No!*" she screamed at him, stepping into the shower and slamming the door hard enough for the glass to rattle. "Let's get something straight. Three years ago you didn't love me—you lusted after me! That's quite a difference! Now you're trying to make a commitment because you're afraid you might be losing that feeling, not because you want me to be your wife, have your children, take care of your house!"

"Are you as dumb as you sound?" he accused through the door. She turned and saw his shadow, then turned back again. Her hands were shaking so badly she could hardly hold the bar of soap. His voice began booming again. "I have a housekeeper—or will have as soon as I find somebody—for the house! I can hire a cook! But you don't hire wives!"

"Right!" she yelled back. "So stop trying to hire me! I'm not someone you can put on hold until you get your career straightened out, then come back to when you have the time! I'm a person! Do you hear? *And I won't marry you!*" By the time she had the nerve and anger built enough to turn around, he was gone.

Then the tears finally came. They blended with the warm water that splashed her skin, keeping the chill she felt so deep inside from forming outside. She stood, head bowed, for a long time, unable to control the small sobs that racked her body.

She had done it. She had set out to make the man
she loved jealous enough to propose, and when he
had, she had thrown his proposal back in his face.
Wanting him to talk of his undying love instead of his
immediate need for shelter from unwanted publicity,
she had shunned his efforts completely. He had proposed and that was all that mattered! And she, like a
stupid fool, had turned him down for all the wrong
reasons! So now, instead of becoming his wife, she
had wrecked any chance of staying his friend and
lover. She had left herself no options, no way out.
What a fool she was! What a great big fool!

Could she undo the damage done? Could she explain her hurt to him so that he would understand and
perhaps forgive her hasty words and confused feelings?

She opened the shower door and frantically reached
under the cupboards for a towel. She wrapped one
around her body and one around her dripping hair,
heedless of the picture she made. Leaving the water
still running, she opened the door to the bedroom.

Jace stood by the closet, his strong tanned body encased in jeans and dark shirt, outlined against the
white of the walls. He had an overnighter in his hand
and was stuffing shirts into it, not bothering to fold
them neatly.

"Jace?" Her voice wobbled as she spoke. She cleared
her throat and tried again. "Jace? What are you doing?"

"I'm leaving," he said as he continued to fill his suitcase. "I'll be gone for a couple of weeks. By that time I
expect you to be moved out of here. When I return I

don't want one thing left to remind me of you." He turned, his face as implacable as stone, his dark eyes blazing at her in anger. "Do you understand? Everything you own is to go with you."

"But—" she began, only to have him interrupt her.

"I'll give you that much time to evict the tenants from your own home or find a place to live and move into it. If you don't find one by then, that's your tough luck, lady. But with your resourcefulness and ingenuity I'm sure you'll find someone else to live with." He slammed the closet door shut, walked past her to the bathroom and collected his shaving gear. His cold voice came to her through a fog of unbelievable, stunning pain. "But don't worry. You probably won't be alone for long. That sexy little body of yours won't let you."

And he walked out of the room, slamming the door behind him. She stood stock-still in the center of the room, her mind reeling at his words, her body feeling bruised and battered. His booted footsteps echoed on the tiled hall. Then she heard the front door slam.

"Jace," she cried, running after him, but she was too late. The car door made a hollow sound as it was closed. By the time she reached the front door, his car engine was echoing down the drive.

"Jace," her lips whispered as she watched the black car turn the corner and heard the motor revving to take the first curve.

Jace had left.

8

BY MONDAY MORNING, April had cried all the tears she had left in her. Her head was stuffed, her eyes rimmed with red and her body felt as if it had been beaten. She looked terrible and didn't care.

Sam glanced up when she walked in the outer reception area, his eyes getting rounder by the second. Dropping the work he had been doing, he followed her into her office and quickly closed the door, letting the part-time girls handle whatever came up for a little while.

"What happened, April? You look awful!" he exclaimed, sitting on the edge of her desk and staring down at her. She could tell by the expression on his face that he had an idea, but he didn't want her to verify it.

"Jace moved out," she said quietly, leaning her head back on the large, leather chair.

"He moved out of his own house?" Sam's eyes grew even larger, if that were possible.

"He's given me two weeks to find someplace else to live." She hesitated, finally saying the words she hadn't wanted to admit, even to herself. "It's over, Sam."

"Damn stupid son of a . . . ." Sam muttered, hitting

the palm of his hand on the top of the desk. "What happened?"

"He proposed and I rejected him."

"But why? Isn't that what you wanted?"

"I did. But he proposed because he didn't want to go out with Sandra Tanner. I lost my temper and blew up." She closed her eyes, seeing the hatred in Jace's eyes once more, and shuddered. "I can't even remember all the circumstances anymore. Things just got all blown out of proportion."

He whistled through his teeth, amazement written on his face. "Now what?" Sam finally asked, breaking the silence. His voice was as quiet as hers.

She sighed, opening her usually bright blue eyes to show that the brilliance had left them. She was so tired. "I don't know. My house is leased for the next four months. I guess I'll start looking around for an apartment in the next day or so. I'm just not up to it right now."

Sam ran an irritated hand through his hair. "It's hard to believe that two of the smartest people I know could be só dumb when it comes to their relationship. I've just lost all faith in love and marriage."

That brought a small smile to her lips, turning them upward to take away the frown she had unconsciously worn. "Liar. You've never believed in either of those institutions, so don't start with the guilt trips now."

Sam had the grace to look slightly sheepish...but only slightly. "I thought you two were different," was his answer.

"So now you know." April felt so lethargic she

could hardly pull herself upright to get to the work on her desk. "So what's new? Anything important?"

Taking her appointment book and turning it around, he glanced down the pages. "You have a palimony case—if the woman shows up," he said, reminding her that most women who arranged appointments for that problem didn't keep them; they made up with their lovers, instead.

"What time?"

"Just before lunch." He looked back at April, his eyes still full of concern. "Then you have a luncheon date."

"With whom?"

"With me."

April smiled again. "You're on."

All her powers of concentration were focused on the appointments of the day. She quickly reviewed her first case. Mrs. Cochran, the woman who had been living with a man, was badly in need of help not only from her lover, but from herself.

The middle-aged woman had taken a job as a housekeeper and then began an affair with the man she was working for. He was obviously not as committed to their relationship as she was. She was living in a dream world, seeing things the way she wanted them to be and not necessarily the way they were.

"Mrs. Cochran, do you understand that the courts will not protect you from your lover unless you move out?" April prodded gently, wondering how anyone could have any feeling left for a man who had treated her so badly she could hardly speak without breaking into tears.

"I know it sounds crazy to you, Ms Flynn. I just want you to talk to him, make him see he could be sued for leading me on and then taking another woman for his wife. He has to see that she isn't the woman who loves him. I am. After all, I'm the one who makes sure he eats right before he goes out, and I do his laundry so that he can date, looking all spiffed up and . . . ." Her voice drifted off at the incredulous expression on April's face.

"You do his laundry so that he can look nice on a date? Mrs. Cochran, what you've given me so far is that you're his housekeeper and you don't want him to marry someone else. Those aren't grounds for a palimony case. We'd be laughed out of court for those reasons." April took a deep breath and began again when she saw the confusion on the older woman's face. "What we need here is evidence that he treated you the way a wife would be treated, introducing you to his friends as his wife, having you hostess for him, living in cohabitation . . . ." Now it was April's turn to drift off in the conversation.

The woman's eyes widened. "I don't think that would work. He's never introduced me as his wife."

April clasped her hands on the desk and leaned toward the other woman, her earnestness finally getting across, she hoped. "Have you made love with him?" she asked, and was patiently silent as Mrs. Cochran's face blushed a deep red before settling back to its natural pallor.

"Yes," the older woman whispered.

"How often?"

Mrs. Cochran looked down at the desk blotter filled with papers. "Twice," she murmured.

April glanced down at her hands. Two times and the woman had worked for him for three years. Some affair! "Recently?"

"No."

April's voice gentled. "And on the basis of those two times you felt he was committed to you?"

"Yes," she murmured, then finally looked up, desperation in her eyes. "He said he had never felt like that with anyone else before! He told me he loved me, and he meant it! I know he did!"

How many times had she heard that? Too many to count. "I'm sure he did at the time. But you see, there isn't enough evidence for a palimony case. There isn't even enough for you to confront him with. Men change their minds about their love life often, Mrs. Cochran, but they can't be sued for it. At least not in this case," April said softly, knowing how awful the woman felt, but also knowing there wasn't any way to patch things up for her. "There is nothing I can do to help you."

The older woman stood and turned, glancing over her shoulder as she left. "Thank you, anyway," she said, crying quietly.

April reached for her pad and pencil. "Wait," she said, scribbling furiously. "I want you to call this woman when you get home and make an appointment to see her. She's a psychologist and adjusts her fees on a sliding scale, according to what you can afford." She ripped off the paper and handed it to the woman. "I want you to tell her what you've told me and talk it out with her." April could tell what was going through Mrs. Cochran's mind from the skeptical look on her face. "Everyone needs someone to talk to sometimes, even if it's just as a sounding board."

Mrs. Cochran's pale-brown eyes seared hers. Then she gave a sharp nod and walked out the door, shutting it quietly behind her.

April cradled her head in her hands. Mrs. Cochran's case had been depressing enough without it underlining the fact that she herself was no better off than her client. Jace had said he loved her, too. But love seemed to be a cheap commodity, used for all the wrong reasons.

Was she in Mrs. Cochran's position, too? Granted she had lived with Jace, but he had made love to her more than . . . twice. And she certainly didn't iron his shirts or feed him more than a bare minimum. In fact, he didn't even support her. She had informed him she would pay the electricity and the phone bills when she moved in. He would look after the mortgage payments and gas bills. Beyond that, at her insistence they usually split the grocery bills. He had always laughed about it. . . .

No, she wasn't a Mrs. Cochran. But she was no better off than her, either. Somehow that notion put a damper on her whole spirit.

The rest of the day passed in a busy blur. April did the work required, went to lunch with Sam, then showed up at court to represent a client's son regarding a neighbor's broken window. After dictating several letters, signing papers and setting up other court dates, she was done for the day.

April sighed, leaning back again to close her eyes, falling into the same position she'd been in when she had begun work that morning. She couldn't remember everything that had happened during the time in between, but she must have done her job, for her out basket was full and her in basket was almost empty.

Sam slipped his head around the door. "Quitting time, counselor. Margarita?"

"I'd love one," she said, not opening her eyes. As long as she kept them closed, Jace was near. She could almost smell his scent, feel his presence in the room. Tears once more prickled her eyelids, and she couldn't believe it. She thought she had cried all the water out of her body.

The blender made a raucous sound, and within seconds after the motor was turned off, a cold glass was slipped into her hand.

"Cheers," Sam said with a gulp, and practically downed his whole drink.

"Cheers," she answered in a monotone, sipping on hers.

"Go out to dinner with me."

"No."

"Why not? You don't have anything better to do," Sam persisted.

"Because you have class tonight and you shouldn't skip it because of me."

"I don't care. Come with me, anyway. I don't want you to be alone," Sam said.

"I've got to get used to it sometime, Sam." She gazed up at him, the hurt and pain showing in her eyes. The rest of her body felt as if it were dead. Perhaps it was. "I think it might as well be now."

He locked eyes with her, telling her in more than

words that he was her friend. But he finally relented. "Call me if you need me? I'll be home by ten tonight."

She nodded. "I will. Now get out of here."

Sam hesitated a minute, then put his glass down on the desk and quietly left.

And April Flynn was alone in the office. She didn't know where she found them, but the burning tears once more cascaded down her cheeks.

She drove home in the dark, after having sat in the office for over an hour when Sam left. Not knowing quite where the strength came from, she had finally picked herself up from the depression she had been in and promised herself to get her act together.

She remembered the scene with Mrs. Cochran and her advice to her. Why could she take care of other people's problems yet couldn't manage her own? Her backbone slowly straightened. But she could. And she would. Determination was in the forefront of her thoughts. Determination to live a full life with or without Jace Sullivan. After all, she had been busy and happy before he had stepped into her life, hadn't she? Of course she had!

Although the house was empty, it echoed with Jace's spirit. But then, what could she expect? It was his house! She fixed a quick meal of an egg sandwich and a glass of milk and perched in front of the television set, needing the voices of people to chase away the memories the house stirred.

At midnight April was in bed. She sprawled in the center, pretending Jace was out of town doing a movie. It didn't work. She was wide awake, her eyes open and staring at the ceiling. She tensed expectantly for a key to turn in the door and Jace's footsteps to echo down the hall. Nothing happened.

A loud birdcall shrilled through the night air and finally she rose. Naked in the moonlight, she dove into the pool and began to swim off her frustrations in the cool water. It wasn't until ten laps and a shower later that her eyes finally closed and she tossed and turned through a light sleep, haunted by dreams of what used to be.

By Thursday April had got herself under control. The tears still came on occasion and the depression hung over her like a pall, but she was bound and determined not to allow it to interfere with her life.

After all, hadn't Jace been bossy with her right from the start? It had taken all her charm, decisiveness, determination and effort to make sure he didn't swallow her whole, absorbing her completely into his life. She had had to fight and often give in on more issues than she really cared to think of, and it was all because he automatically expected to be the leader in their two-man parade. Well, that wasn't how it worked!

For the past week she had remembered small incidents that had begun to feed her newfound anger, and in remembering them over and over, she found the methods she could use to fight her way out of this blackness that seemed to overwhelm her at times.

She pulled into the driveway late Thursday, after stopping at a fast-food drive-in on the way home. She had eaten with one hand while steering with the other. The wrappings were the only clue to what she had ordered. That could easily have been toothpicks and straw for all that she'd tasted, but it was better than eating at home. She couldn't face having to practice her meager cooking skills on just herself.

The lights were on. A mixture of surprise, fear and excitement coursed through her veins as she realized that Jace must be there. Her step was livelier, her mind ready for a fight. Finally getting the chance to tell Jace what she thought of his walking away from their commitment, no matter that it wasn't sanctioned by marriage, put a sparkle in her blue eyes.

The door was locked. Had he tried to lock her out? No, he wouldn't do that on purpose. He'd given her two weeks to find another place, and she knew that he'd honor that agreement. She struggled with the keys, finally opening the door, only to be greeted by the hollow sound of silence.

"Who's here," she called. No one answered.

With slow steps she walked into the hallway, then into the living room, flicking on more lights as she went. Still no one.

She knew without checking further that there was no one in the house.

Suddenly all the spirit was gone from her, and she felt drained and empty. Her heart thumped heavily in her breast in sympathy to her feelings of loss. She sat down on the couch, despondently dropping her head in her hands. He had been here, but he had gone without saying anything, giving anything, asking her to give anything.

The tears started again. She sniffed, then swallowed the lump that had formed in her throat. This time she refused to let them fall. With determined steps she walked to the phone and began dialing.

Her voice shook as she spoke, and she could only hope he couldn't hear it from his end of the phone. "Sam? Care to have a free night on the town? My treat. Any delicacy you want."

With alarming quickness he agreed, and she arranged to pick him up in an hour. That gave her thirty minutes to get ready and thirty minutes for the drive to his duplex. Suddenly she was moving at a fever pitch, anxious to leave the very place that reminded her of Jace.

It wasn't until she was dressed and looking in the mirror across from the bed that she realized there was a note propped up on her pillow.

With shaking hands she reached for it, opening the flap and pulling out a sheet of her own paper.

Flynn, had to pick up a few of my clothes. Left the light on for you. If you need anything, call me at the studio.

Jace

"If I *need* anything!" she exclaimed to the ceiling in a voice heavily laced with tears. "If I *need* anything...." With shaking hands she tore the note to shreds, letting the ripped pieces fall carelessly on the dark carpeting like pristine snowflakes on a chocolate ground.

She took deep breaths, trying hard to calm her rising sense of hysteria. But the hysteria wouldn't stay away. Suddenly she was laughing and crying all at once. She didn't *need* anything! She *wanted*! She wanted his arms around her, his lips on hers, his body deliciously covering hers with touches and kisses. She wanted to feast her eyes on his tall, firm frame. She wanted his husky laughter, his gripes, his silent moments and his bad cooking. But above all, she wanted his presence in her life again.

Looking around, she was constantly reminded of Jace. His furniture. His books. His clothing. His house. She had to get out of here. April grabbed her purse and frantically searched for her keys. With them in hand, she ran down the corridor and out the door, slamming and locking it with jerky movements.

Sam was waiting at his apartment, watching the last of a football game on television. One look at her face and he turned off the TV.

In silence he poured a glass of straight Scotch and had her sip it. She did, almost enjoying the burning sensation that took the pain away from her heart for just a few minutes. He led her to the couch, perching her there while he fiddled with the dials of the stereo, giving her time to get herself under control.

She leaned back, her eyes imploring him for an answer. "I can't go back there tonight, Sam. I can't think. I can't sleep. What do I do?"

He turned, smiling sadly. "Stay here."

Her eyes rounded. "Here?"

"Why not? I have an extra bedroom."

She sighed, leaning back and closing her eyes. "Thanks," she murmured before glancing up at him once more.

He stood at the edge of the couch, looking down with concern etched on his face and in his eyes. His hand involuntarily came out to rake a dark lock of hair back from her face.

She smiled. "Don't you want to know what happened?"

He grinned again. "As a good attorney, I'll always get to the bottom of things. As a good friend, I'll wait until you're ready to tell me. I know the difference."

"Thank you, Sam."

Relaxing in his calming company, April stretched out and leaned her head back in weariness.

Without asking her, Sam called a pizza place that delivered and within twenty minutes had their fare served up on a paper plate. They ate mostly in silence; occasional conversation began and was then abandoned. When she was finished, he took her plate and left her to the empty room while he puttered around the kitchen.

"Will I live through this?" she asked the ceiling.

The answer came from the vicinity of the kitchen door. "You'd better, April. You're going to be my partner in law, whether you like it or not!"

"Yes, sir!" She couldn't help but grin at him, although her smile was a watery one. He was so good to her and for her, and she wondered, not for the first time, how she ever had the good luck to hire him.

She didn't know the point at which she drifted off to sleep, but her eyelids felt as if lead weights were attached to them. Her mind wrapped itself in fog, and with it came the blessed release of built-up tensions.

She didn't know what time it was when Sam gently

shook her shoulders and, against her tired will, led her to bed. He slipped off her shoes, unzipped her dress and let her tumble between the cool sheets with her slip as a gown. Covering her up, he smiled, but his eyes were tinged with sadness. She had come to him because she was in love with another man. She had confided in him because he was her friend. In all their time working together, she had never thought of him in any other context. She didn't love him. She loved Jace.

Thus began a new pattern. April arrived from Sam's apartment to the office, worked until she was so tired she dropped, then ate a quick meal before Sam took off for class and she met him back at his apartment.

They would sometimes share a meal together, but most nights Sam came home as April was straightening up the apartment before going to bed.

One night Sam arrived early, just as April was puttering around after a long soaking bath. Her terrycloth robe was belted tightly, her hair still damp and clinging to her head.

"Don't tell me you didn't take a girl out tonight?"

"Yes, I did."

"Then what happened? You shouldn't be home for at least another hour or two."

Her eyes twinkled with sparkling blue lights the way they used to, and Sam had to clear his voice before he could speak. "She was too boring to carry on a conversation with for more than a few minutes. Besides, she lived with two other roommates, and I couldn't very well bring her to my home."

The smile was wiped from April's face as she realized just how much her living at Sam's was interfering with his own life. "Oh, Sam! I'm sorry. I never even gave a thought to your, your . . . you know."

He chuckled at her apparent dismay. "Don't worry. If she had been worth spending time with, I would have brought her home and asked you to retire. But this girl had no brains. I think God gave her helium, instead, because she was certainly filled with nothing else. One big airhead," he said disgustedly. "To tell you the truth, if you weren't here, I think I might have invented your being here, just so she couldn't come in."

"You mean she suggested coming here?" April still wasn't sure she hadn't cramped Sam's style.

"Oh, yes," he said as he sat heavily in the overstuffed leather chair across from her. "She didn't suggest, she told me over dinner she thought we should be at my apartment before nine because she had to leave at ten-thirty and get home to bed. She also wanted to know if I thought that would be time enough for me to take her to 'ecstasy,' as she called it. I told her she was too much woman for me and dropped her off at her house."

A giggle escaped April's mouth, to be joined by Sam's deep, rueful chuckle. Soon they were both belly-laughing at the picture of the girl giving her estimation of a "good date."

"I don't know where you find some of them, Sam. You seem to have so much sense when it comes to everything else."

He shrugged. "They're diversions. Some of the girls

I date are really neat ladies in their own right. Some are just nice ordinary girls, and then occasionally one comes along like this one. Thank God, I don't run into them very often."

"But when you do, you don't need a roommate to scare them away," she said, sobering as she realized the spot she had put him in. "I need to find a place of my own."

"You don't, either. I enjoy having you here, and if I want to bring someone home, I'll let you know," Sam stated emphatically, but April's eyes already showed her decision.

"We'll see," she said as she unwrapped her legs and stood, walking slowly down the hallway. "Good night, Sam."

"Good night, April." Sam sat in the chair and watched her retreat down the hall to her bedroom. Then he closed his eyes and tried to redirect his thoughts to something other than the pain that April was feeling.

APRIL HAD PICKED UP SOME CLOTHING from Jace's house just shortly after moving into Sam's. Then just as quickly as she could, she had left. It was almost as if she were afraid of the ghosts of good times reminding her again of what she had lost. The rest of her belongings were there, but she hadn't broken the lease the tenants of her house had signed and hadn't found an apartment to put her things in. Every time she thought of it, she'd push that prospect aside, using work as an excuse. She couldn't seem to find the strength to make the final break of packing her things. It was as if there were some slim thread of hope as long as her belongings were still in his house.

Jace's picture was in the paper again. He was escorting Sandra Tanner to a Hollywood charity ball. He was smiling and Sandra was radiant. All the columns were guessing at their relationship; most were hinting at the peal of wedding bells in their future.

April read all the newspapers. Jace was like an aching cavity she kept testing with her tongue. Each piece of news hurt more than the last, but she couldn't stop reading. She kept hoping that with all the information at hand, she would finally come to realize that their relationship was over and he was gone.

But her dreams continued to show her the good side of their love. They focused on the tender and fun times and kept the flame of hope alive enough at night to feed her growing despondency in the light of day.

Now she knew what Catch 22 really meant.

April looked at the calendar on her desk to check if she had any more court dates for next week. With an intense pain that shot through her like a sharp arrow, she realized that if everything had gone according to schedule, Jace's movie commitment would end today. She held her stomach as if it were bleeding. They were supposed to leave for their secluded cabin in Oregon on Saturday. Tomorrow. It was to have been a magic time for them, with no one around to monitor movements or actions. It was to have been their time. . . .

Saturday. Her shoulders stiffened and her throat closed, making it hard to breathe.

She'd had so many high hopes at the beginning of the month. Oh, how she had playfully schemed to get Jace to propose to her! What wonderfully high expectations she had held for their life. Their dreams. Their love. But they couldn't even weather the storm of disagreement, let alone the tempest of jealousy and desire.

Deep down inside she had to face the fact that she had wanted him to change her mind about not accepting his proposal. Like all Prince Charmings, he was supposed to have talked her out of her angry mood with kisses and caresses, making her acquiesce to his stronger will. Then she would have allowed herself to succumb to his charms, having been wooed and cooed into his plans.

She had been playing games, something she had never before done in their relationship, and it had boomeranged on her. Oh, how it had boomeranged! By behaving so stupidly, she had lost everything she had ever wanted, and all because she had been playing games!

First thing Saturday morning she found a place to live. It had been easy; there had been a small Apartments For Rent sign just across the street from her office. She placed first and last month's rent down and made herself a list of things to do that included going back to Jace's house for her belongings. The list made her moving out seem more like fact, and she stared at it, knowing then that all was real: she had lost Jace.

Midafternoon, April forced herself to climb in her

car and head for the canyon. She had a few empty boxes in the back seat along with a piece of empty luggage. It was time.

TWO WEEKS HAD DRAGGED BY with agonizing slowness for Jace. The film was now in the can and he'd completed the details of his contract. He spent most of his time around the hotel bar, sipping on drinks and dreaming of what might have been. Until Saturday.

By eleven that morning he was in his mother's rented home in Bel Air, a posh neighborhood filled with movie and rock stars' homes.

He stood facing the front bay window as he waited for his mother to come downstairs and see him. His mind came up with so many good lines he could say when she walked in, but none of them was spoken when she entered and he turned toward her.

"Hello, mother."

She stood in the living-room doorway in an expensive ecru wrap, her dark hair tumbling down her back. The expression on her face was one of mingled hope and fear. "Good morning, Jace. Is everything okay?"

"Of course it is." His irritation rose to the surface. She didn't know him well enough to read him so clearly. It wasn't right.

His mother's back straightened, and her eyes narrowed much the way his did when he was angry. "If I want to be spoken to in that way again, I'll look you up. Meanwhile, if that's the tone you have in mind for our conversation, then I hope you'll understand if I say I don't want to waste my morning hearing it."

For a minute she reminded him of April when she was angry, but her eyes were spitting as much obstinacy and fire as Jace's.

Suddenly he saw himself, and his shoulders slumped. One shaky hand ran through his dark hair. "I'm sorry. I didn't mean to bark at you." He gave a wry grin. "I'm not doing too well at making peace, am I?"

Erica took a few steps into the room. "Make peace? You came here for that?"

"Yes. I had a long look at myself and decided it was time for a few changes. One of them was to make peace with you. It seems imperative if we're going to live in the same city with each other," he added awkwardly, as if seeking a legitimate excuse for his being in her home.

She closed her eyes tight as if to keep the tears at bay. When she opened them, they were suspiciously bright. She stared at him for a minute. Then her hands came out in an arc as if to reach out to him, only to fall at her sides. "I don't know what to say."

For the first time Jace grinned boyishly. "Neither do I," he replied, keeping the lump in his throat from interfering with his voice. "I just know I had a few things to clear up, and this was one."

"Did April suggest this?" Erica asked, her mind still obviously reeling from all that was happening.

"No," Jace said quietly. The lump grew bigger. "She suggested making peace with my past, but this visit was my own idea."

"She's a smart woman. It would be nice if we could all make peace with the past. It seems to have a major bearing on the future," she said. She took another hesitant step forward, then stepped back again, suddenly smiling disarmingly at him. "So if we're going to make peace, why don't we do it over a cup of coffee? It will keep my hands busy, and you'll be able to talk without looking directly at me."

He chuckled, relieved that they would be doing something. The meeting was so much more awkward than he had thought it would be, as if both of them were strangers trying to find a bond between them. "Is that why the British always make tea in time of crisis?" he asked as he followed her down the large gallery.

"I don't know, but it makes sense."

Three hours later he was on his way to Sid's office. Funny how quickly time could pass.

April had been right; he had magnified everything that had to do with the relationship between his mother and him, and it had taken this long to begin to come to terms with this.

For the first time in his adult life, he asked halting questions about her career and what she had been doing when he was born. And he asked about the relationship between his father and her. And she more than eagerly answered.

They talked of angers that had built up over the death of his father. It seemed that each had looked at his demise as if it were an affront to them singly, instead of together. That was when the real split had come. They had both held back that anger for fear of hurting the other, until the abyss had become so large they couldn't cross it with mere words . . . then. Now, perhaps with time, they would at least be able to think of each other without feeling the bitterness between them.

There were so many things he understood now, as an adult, that he could never have understood as a child. Things such as the lack of money, the ambition for a successful career that had taken them all over the globe, the relationships with men for both comfort and security. He no longer had to judge, just listen and understand. And in some ways her answers were his own answers. It was amazing.

His thoughts flew to April and how many parallels there were between his relationship with her and his mother's relationships with others. His mother had been just as afraid to make a commitment as he had after his own disastrous marriage. They had both decided that getting hurt once was enough. His mother hadn't realized that hurt was part of love. But Jace knew.

The more he listened to his mother, the more he saw himself and realized just how selfish he had been in his relationship with April. He had expected her to give everything, while he gave only what he wanted to and no more.

At the thought of losing April for good, a deep pain began in his stomach and circled through his limbs. He had to get her back and make her understand he had changed. He realized now just how much he needed the same things she did: love, marriage, children, commitment. And perhaps with her help he could become all the good things she thought he was. He fervently prayed for another chance. . . .

He pulled into the parking lot and handed his car over to the attendant. Pocketing his keys, he stepped quickly into the large five-story building and took the elevator to Sid's office. He had a few more things to do before he could face April and win her back.

Jace stood in Sid's office, moodily staring at the blowup of Charlie Chaplin but seeing, instead, April's face as she had looked when he proposed.

Sid's voice droned on, but none of the words registered. Until Sandra's name was mentioned.

"What!" he exclaimed, turning on his agent as if he were a rattler in high grass.

Sid smoothed the remaining few hairs on his head, patting them to reassure himself they were still in place. "I said that on Sunday night you're supposed to take Sandra to a small but well-publicized dinner party at your director's house."

"In a pig's eye," Jace stated through gritted teeth. "First of all, I'm supposed to be on vacation starting today. One whole month off, remember?" Suddenly a pain so intense it almost doubled him over seared through his body. He was supposed to be with April. He was supposed to be proposing marriage.... He shook himself. "Besides, I've had about all I can handle with that female space cadet, and now that the movie's in the can, I'm through with her."

Sid raised his brow. "I thought you two were getting along nicely."

"I'm an actor, remember?"

"Then you and Miss Flynn are back together?"

Jace faced the poster of Charlie Chaplin again.

"That has nothing to do with this. I took Sandra everywhere I was supposed to, and now my debt has been paid and the studio owes me one—the right to produce the script I want."

"Which is?"

"*Goodbye, Spring.*"

Sid didn't really look surprised this time. "Did you know that your mother wants to play the sister?"

Jace's brows rose. Then he shrugged, his eyes straying around the room instead of looking directly at his agent. "Erica would be good in the part. I don't give a damn whether she's my mother. I just want a good script with good actors. One that will prove I can act in something besides light comedy. I think this is the part that will do it."

Sid whistled low through his teeth. "You really haven't been yourself lately, have you?"

Jace turned, his brows drawn together. "What do you mean by that?"

"I mean," Sid said slowly, ignoring the stormy looks he was receiving, "that everyone you've worked with the past two weeks has been walking on glass whenever you're around. They've been saying you've lost your sense of humor and your insight into other people. Now it seems you've lost your animosity for Erica, when you've refused to be civil to her for years. Will wonders never cease?"

"Look, Sid," Jace began, only to have his agent raise a small, well-manicured hand to ward off the harsh words he knew were coming.

"I'm only repeating what I've been hearing, Jace. Don't get in an uproar about it. I've noticed the changes, too, and wondered what was going on. You're not only my client, you're a friend."

"A friend wouldn't listen to gossip."

"A friend would not only listen but pass it on so that you'd know what others weren't willing to say to your face."

Jace walked over to the wing leather chair and slumped into it, suddenly exhausted from all the sparring he had done in the past two weeks. Sid was right; he had been almost impossible to work with lately, and it had been only the gentle persuasion of the cast that had allowed them to finish the film on schedule. He was seeing himself as everyone else had lately, and what he saw, he didn't like. But all that was changing. . . .

"Sorry," he said, a clip in his voice even though he knew he should be more gracious. After all, Sid wasn't in the wrong. He was.

Sid leaned back, narrowing his eyes through his glasses in order to catch Jace's every expression.

"Do you love her?"

Jace looked up, surprised at the question. Sid had never got so personal before. "Yes," he finally admitted aloud.

"Did you tell her so?"

"Hundreds of times."

"Then why didn't you marry her?"

Jace was quiet for a moment before answering. He had never tried to put his reasons into words before, and he found it hard, though comforting, to do so now. "I never had to dangle that carrot in front of any woman before. I honestly thought that I was in charge and that if she wanted me she'd have to take me on my terms or not at all. It was a kind of a game, where I was the prize and the victor all at the same time. Others had succumbed to my charms, and, by damn, so would she."

"And she did," Sid finished dryly.

"Yes, but it wasn't the same. I thought about proposing for a long time but always put it off for the perfect circumstances. And when I finally did it was all wrong."

"I take it she wasn't bowled over?"

Jace grinned at the memory of her face in the pool as she worked off her frustrations. She had hated him then, but she had also desired him. It was evident in both her glance and her sensuous moves. Yet against his rising desires, he had chosen to play the hurt suitor and had left her there, instead of scooping her up in his arms and taking her to his bed, where they both belonged. He could have changed her way of thinking; he knew that. He could have brought her around so that she was as pliable as melted taffy. Yet how could he explain the immense hurt he felt when she hurled his proposal back in his face? He had *known* it wasn't the right time and the right circumstances, but still...it hurt. It ached like hell. But that was no excuse for his actions. "She wasn't bowled over, but I could have tried harder to persuade her."

"But you didn't want to lower yourself to that, did you?"

"No. I wanted her to succumb totally. Again." He looked up at his friend and agent. "Stupid?" he asked with a wry sadness, knowing the answer before Sid slowly nodded his head in agreement.

"But the young are famous for making mistakes. It isn't until you become my age that you can see all the right answers to all the wrong questions." Sid's voice held a teasing note, for he wasn't but ten or so years older than Jace.

"It must be nice to watch us mortals from your lofty perch."

Sid nodded again. "Entertaining, to say the least."

"Well, how about coming down from the mountain long enough to have drinks and dinner at my place? I bake a mean potato and grill a mean steak."

"You don't have anything better to do on a Saturday?" Sid asked. "Besides, I thought you weren't at your place anymore."

"It's time to move back." Jace spoke with steel in his voice. "I've been hiding at the Beverly Wilshire, but that's over. I'm just as lonely there as I would be at home. Besides, I've made a few decisions lately about my personal life. I'm going after what I want, though first I have to figure how to do it."

"How about saying, 'I'm sorry'?"

"Don't be cute," Jace chided him. "Come with me and help me figure it out, instead."

Sid sighed. "Okay, but let me call the studio and tell them where you'll be. You might work a five-day week, but the studio doesn't. I wasn't going to tell you, but they're making their decision about *Goodbye, Spring* today."

Jace looked surprised. "So you knew all along."

"Of course. When you contacted them, they contacted me. You need someone to negotiate for you. Why not me?"

Sid was nothing if not logical. Jace stood quietly for a minute, waiting for the glee of getting the role to flood him. But nothing happened. What had been so important a month ago had lost a lot of its glitter. Success didn't taste as sweet without Flynn. Right now, he had to find a way back to Flynn, or nothing would have the fine taste of success.

"Let's go," Jace said, rising from his seat and heading toward the door. "I'll drive you back to your car later."

9

APRIL PARKED HER CAR in the garage and walked around the front of the house, as if this were the beginning ritual of saying goodbye with her eyes and her heart. With a sense of finality, she stood at the opened door of Jace's house, her key in her hand. Although the house echoed with the silence, the ghosts of loving times were everywhere. They were crammed in the hallway, making her realize how many times she had returned home to find Jace there, standing and waiting for her with a kiss.

The entry to the living room reminded her of those moments they had stood, waiting to dissolve into each other's arms, holding and caring the day's tensions away. They had often made love on the couch or on the plush carpeting in front of the large stucco fireplace, teasing each other with words and shared laughter, as well as kisses and caresses. . . .

Her hand tightened around the key, and her heart thumped with the primitive needs her thoughts had provoked.

Playing games, playing games, her mind repeated over and over. It was really all her fault for playing games. She had run, and had expected him to chase her. She had turned him down when he had finally done what she had prayed for him to do. She had acted the outraged lover when he had wanted her to be the only woman in his life. She was the fool, not Jace.

Was it too late? Did Jace feel the loss as much as she did? Was he as sorry as she was and couldn't find the words to tell her so? He had done that once before. Perhaps the same emotions held him back now. How could she tell him she was sorry for her hasty words and make up with him? Go to his hotel? No, she'd be crushed if she found him not there or in someone else's arms. Besides, she didn't have the faintest idea where he was staying!

She pushed aside the thought that had crept insidiously in—that he might be staying with one of the many women who dogged his steps...perhaps even Sandra Tanner. He wouldn't do that. He would return to his own home and then move the woman in, not the other way around.

Perhaps April should call him at the studio and ask him to meet her. No, she couldn't stand it if he said no. Then how? There had to be some way for her to confront Jace without his gaining time to place a steel wall between them. She had to catch him off guard. Only then would he be surprised enough to listen to what she had to say.

The phone rang and she automatically picked it up, her mind on her problem.

"Is Mr. Sullivan there?" April recognized the studio secretary's voice, and her heart did a flip-flop.

"No. May I take a message?" Her voice sounded so cool and self-assured. Perhaps she should have gone into acting, too.

"Please ask him to call Mr. Hargrove's office as soon as he comes in," the woman answered crisply.

"I'll leave a message, but I'm not sure when he'll return."

"I'd appreciate that. I called his agent's office and his secretary said Mr. Sullivan had left for his home a short time ago."

Again April felt the flip-flop, only this time in joy. Jace was coming! By the time she placed the phone in its cradle, she was fervently planning their meeting.

She closed her eyes and held her breath. Crossing her fingers, she made an ardent wish. *Let him listen, let him listen. . . .*

She was staying. She would catch Jace, explain her actions to him and throw herself at his feet. Well . . . maybe not "throw" herself, but she *would* apologize. After all, it was her fault that she had brought game playing into their relationship. Jace had always been honest and up-front, had never resorted to such manipulations. Well, almost never. Then she would be sweet and generous when it was his time to apologize. He could at least say he knew he was an arrogant bastard for expecting her to be grateful for the proposal he had offhandedly thrown her way.

With excitement flowing through her veins like high-voltage electricity, she quickly ran into the bedroom, pushing hangers this way and that until she found what she was looking for. As she pulled out an old red-velvet skirt, a smile began to curve her mouth.

Next she searched frantically in her drawer, sighing with relief when she found the scissors. Placing them carefully on the carpet and taking careful measure, she slit the skirt up the seamed side so that it was one large piece of material. Then she folded it in half and carefully cut out one half of a heart.

Holding it up, she could hardly contain the giggle that passed her slightly parted lips. It was perfect! The top half-moons barely covered the tips of her breasts. The tip of the heart came down just enough to hide the vee of her long legs. Now where was the silver glitter and glue she had used last year at Christmas?

She found them in the kitchen catch-all drawer. Stretching the material out on the table, she wrote *I love you* in glue, then sprinkled the silver speckles over it. After she dusted the loose sparkles into the trash can, she took another look.

The silver-glittered script writing was a perfect foil for the deep ruby red of the heart. For a quick job, it didn't look bad. As a matter of fact, she thought, examining it with a critical eye, it looked darned good!

Now on to step two. . . .

April had just got out of the shower and dried herself off when she heard the dull roar of a car engine. After three years of listening for it, she'd know that sound anywhere! Jace's Alfa Romeo was on the last patch of road leading up to the driveway. She quickly dusted the expensive bath powder over her skin and, after a quick glance in the steaming mirror to check her hair, ran to the red velvet heart lying on the bed.

Her plan was to greet him in the hallway, so she would have to hurry if she was to be in the correct spot on time.

She practically flew down the hall in her bare feet.

Taking a deep breath, she stopped, waiting expectantly, her mouth delightfully curving up at the corners as she anticipated his surprise. She just prayed she didn't encounter his scowl, instead.

Suddenly there were two voices at the front door, and the hot blood shooting through her veins turned to ice. Her legs were leaden with shock and her brain seemed to have atrophied. Two people! Now what? Frantic, she looked around the empty hallway for something to hide behind, but there was nothing. The key slipped into the lock, the knob rattled and someone slowly opened the door. . . .

JACE HAD DRIVEN like a maniac all the way up the canyon road. He had no idea why—perhaps excess energy now that he had decided on his course of action—but he finally did slow down when he noticed the ashen-gray face of his agent. Sid looked as if he were murmuring his last prayers and mentally checking his will.

Jace knew what his problem was: he was afraid of seeing if April had moved her belongings out and had changed his home from an enchanted house back into an ordinary dwelling. He wanted to know, needed to know, in case he could glean some hope for their relationship. But he also liked his ignorance. He really dreaded opening the door, in case she had moved out. With Sid there it was going to be hard to take the physical evidence of her no longer being in his home, but at least he knew he wouldn't break down in front of the other man. Sid was his insurance for acting like Mr. Cool—at least for a while.

But what happens when you find she's gone and Sid leaves, too, his mind taunted, and he knew the answer without putting it into words. He would tear the town apart until he found her, sling her over his shoulder, take her to their cabin in the mountains and make love to her until she *had* to marry him!

He had watched her enough over the past week to know that she was staying with Sam at his duplex. Lucky for Sam he was still dating, if his evening trips out were anything to go by. If Sam had stayed home with her, Jace would have torn him limb from limb. As long as he was still dating, Jace knew that April was safe. April might not believe that Sam was romantically inclined toward her, but Jace would bet his next residual check that if Sam thought there was a chance April would fall in love with him, he'd take it.

Since it was only afternoon there were no lights on in the house, which was good, for he didn't want to see it dark and empty. He roared up the driveway and screeched to a halt, for a minute forgetting Sid and his last-minute will. The driveway was empty. Hell! What did he expect? Flynn waiting at the door with a drink and a loving smile? The thought of what he had lost through his own pride only made him angrier. Only now the anger was directed where it should have been: at himself.

"Am I going to be subjected to this mood for the rest of the day?" Sid asked as they walked across the drive and toward the front door.

Jace muttered something under his breath before giving a sigh and a sheepish smile. "Sorry. I was thinking of how I'm going to haul her back here."

"You'll come up with something original, I'm sure," Sid replied dryly. "My question is—does the lady *want* to be in your life?"

"I don't know, but I don't think I'm going to give her the chance to make that decision. She'll be mine if I have to hog-tie her!" His last word was spoken as he opened the front door and stood aside to usher Sid in.

"That ought to be interesting. I've never seen you have to struggle to gain a woman's attention before. She must have really knocked you on your... knees."

Jace smiled for the first time that afternoon. "I promise I'll try to be better company. I have a plan of action now, and I can concentrate on being a good host," he said solemnly. "Besides, I can't lose my best agent's good blessing," he said, reaching for Sid's very proper suit jacket as he shrugged out of it. "Here, let me take that for you."

He turned to the hall closet and opened the door, automatically reaching for the coat hangers April always made sure were in there. Instead his hand encountered warm flesh and registered that fact even before his eyes focused enough to see the owner of the softly rounded breast he now palmed.

"Hi," April said in a very quiet, subdued voice. Her face as well as her body almost matched the flame red of the heart that barely covered her.

"April?" Jace uttered, his tone ending on a high note.

"Hello, Miss Flynn," Sid said very properly and with a straight face, holding out his hand. "I don't know if you remember me, but I've met you before, on, uh, other occasions. I'm Jace's agent."

April began to reach for his hand until she realized the dilemma she was in. The heart needed two hands to stay in place. Tucking the top of the velvet material under her arm, she bent slightly forward, exposing a delectable cleavage, and shook his hand. "I remember. How are you, Sid?" She barely managed a glance at Jace's still-astonished face. "I bet you're wondering what I'm doing here. . . ." Her blue eyes darted back and forth again, seeing Jace's scowl deepen even more so that his eyebrows looked like one dark slash. She quickly glanced away, only to encounter Sid's appreciative gaze. Once more she blushed a violent red from head to toe, backing farther into the closet as if she could escape their scrutiny.

"I can't wait to hear your explanation, but wouldn't it be easier for us to talk if you stepped out of the closet and into the hallway? I promise I'll try hard not to appear too lecherous," Sid teased, both delighted and amused at the predicament they all found themselves in. It promised to be a most entertaining evening if Jace's expression of utter disbelief was any indication.

"Get that coat on," Jace ordered, finally finding his tongue. He reached behind her and pulled his old khaki trench coat off the hanger, thrusting it into her arms before he quickly shut the door in her face.

His agent couldn't seem to control himself any longer. Sid stood where he was, unable to move and belly-laugh at the same time. Tears streamed down his cheeks. The more he laughed, the angrier Jace became, and the more Sid laughed. For a slight man, his laughter was a loud and deep baritone, and it seemed to echo in Jace's ears.

"Would you please get the hell into the living room, Sid, while I straighten this out?" Jace ran a hand through his hair, staring at the now-closed closet as if he had X-ray vision and knew what April was doing in there.

"Straighten what out?" Sid asked innocently between gulps of air, but his eyes had a knowing twinkle.

"One more laugh from you and I'll set you on your ear," Jace threatened as he tried to act as a shield between Sid and the hall door he was about to open again. "Pour yourself a drink and calm down. I'll be there in a minute," he ordered, his hand on the knob.

Jace and Sid could both hear the thuds and groans as April struggled in the confined closet space, apparently trying to get her arms through the coat sleeves.

Sid rubbed the tears from his eyes and reluctantly walked across the hall. "Okay, but remember. You're the one who just ten minutes ago was trying to find a way to capture her. I'd say you caught her. Don't look a gift horse in the mouth, Jace. You might be sorry."

Jace counted to ten, then opened the closet door slowly, anticipating a hand reaching out to slap his face or push by him, or perhaps an empty closet and the whole thing in his imagination.

April stood in the opening, the too-large trench

coat wrapped around her waist and the belt tied in a knot. Her dark-brown hair had fallen in her face, forming delightful bangs that highlighted the brightness of her eyes. Her face was colored with apprehension; the brilliant blue of her eyes already glistened with tears. But her chin was tilted proudly and her mouth was straight with grit.

"I embarrassed you," she said softly but with earnestness. "I'm sorry. I didn't know you were bringing company home, uh, to your house. If you'll move aside, I'll get into my clothes and leave."

Jace still held the door, his arm acting as a fence. "Not so fast. What were you doing here?" His voice was deep yet grating, as if he were truly angry.

"I—I'm not sure anymore," she confessed in a shaky whisper. "It was a stupid, crazy idea that hit me and, and I thought it would work, but it didn't. As usual, it backfired."

"What was it supposed to accomplish?" His tone was almost conversational, but the scowl was still creasing his forehead.

"Let me out, please. I'll call you tomorrow and discuss this if you feel you need answers. Right now—" she stopped and took a deep breath, her eyes silently pleading "—right now, I just want to leave here."

"Not until you answer me. What were you doing in there? What are you doing here?"

"All right! I was going to surprise you so you wouldn't be able to erect that wall you were building between us. I wanted you to hear my side of this crazy relationship before you had a chance to think.

Instead, I think you were right all along. We shouldn't be together. You need your own 'space,' and I'll, I'll. . . ." Her voice broke. Without waiting for him to move, she quickly ducked under his arm and ran down the hallway toward the bedroom, the long trench coat making a flapping noise as it hit against her ankles.

She closed the door and flipped the lock. It was flimsy at best, but if he tried to follow at least he would realize she really did want to be alone. The message she was giving with the lock and the message her heart thumped with every beat were entirely different, but she had made enough of a fool of herself today without doing more harm.

She dressed quickly, throwing on dark-blue cords and a blue-and-purple-striped silk shirt. As she ran a brush through her hair she heard a car, but since she knew the sound of Jace's, she dismissed the noise. Besides, he wouldn't be gentleman enough to leave her here to disappear with her own misery. Knowing Jace, he'd want to exact his pound of flesh and have a good laugh at the same time. Well, the flesh was owed, but the laughter she didn't deserve!

Throwing clothes into her empty suitcase and the few boxes she had retrieved from the back of her car, she piled them next to the door. The rest of her things would have to stay in the house a while longer. The quicker she got away, the better off she'd be.

Fifteen minutes later she was ready to leave. For just a minute she indulged herself and leaned her head against the cool wood of the door. How dumb could she have been! If one of her clients had seen her, they would have laughed her out of court!

And Jace! Jace was furious with her, and she didn't blame him. Now she was just like all the other women who had flung themselves at his feet. She had made the biggest error of all: she had allowed him to take away her pride as well as her heart.

She pulled herself erect. If she could just leave with a little dignity now, she could break down later. She promised herself that relief.

With sweating palms she opened the door and peeked around the corner down the hall, finally ready to confront Jace and his agent. Instead there was only Jace.

He was sitting on a chair he had apparently pulled from the dining room, holding the heart she had so quickly made. Her mouth dropped open.

His clothing was in a neat pile next to the door. All of it, including his dark knit underwear, which lay on top of his pants. She glanced at him again. He was stark naked. He looked at her, then back down to the heart he held in his hands, staring at it as if it held more of a message than she had written. Then his brown eyes focused on her, pinning her feet to the doorway floor. "Do you mean this? Really mean this?"

"Sure." She shrugged as if she didn't care. "I always leave scarlet hearts and letters just before I end relationships. It makes it easier."

He ignored her sarcasm, his eyes still burning a hole through her. "Then why did you refuse my proposal. Didn't you think I meant it?"

She waited before answering. Then, with a slump of her shoulders, she decided that playing games had got her into enough trouble. It was time for the truth. "I thought you were using me as a shield and it hurt my pride. I've wanted to marry you ever since we met, but you were against it."

"I wouldn't have proposed if I were so against it, Flynn. I would have ranted and raved, but not proposed. I've been planning to ask you for the past several months, but I wanted the surroundings to be right for us." He hesitated before going on in a low, deep voice, his feelings plain. "I had imagined us sitting before a roaring fire in the cabin in Oregon, drinking champagne. I dreamed of it so often it almost seemed as if I had already done it and you had said yes. I had the whole thing planned.... Then I blew it by saying the wrong things at the wrong time for all the wrong reasons." His face showed the honesty of his words and her heart beat faster. She was afraid to experience the joy she felt, but unable to contain the hope that abounded in her breast. "I had meant to tell you how much I loved you, how much you meant to me and will always mean to me."

"Really?" she said, afraid to take his words at value until he reassured her.

Jace stood, placing the cloth heart on the chair. He took two steps toward her, his nakedness more a barrier than his clothing would have been. He was so vulnerable, so very masculine, so damn handsome. "Oh, really, Flynn," he mocked. "I told myself I was always honest where relationships with women were concerned, but I was just kidding myself. I played

games with you...and with me. The funny thing
was that I didn't even realize it until recently. Losing
you was the worst thing that ever happened to me,
but it also made me take a good look at myself." His
hands found her waist and clung to her hips. There
were just a few inches between them, but the air was
filled with heat. "I wanted to bend you to my will so
we would both know who was boss." He grated a
laugh at himself. "Some joke, when you were having
your way all along."

"Oh," she said softly, her blue eyes glowing.
"When?"

He chuckled ruefully. "Always. Every time I tried
to act the big macho movie star, you'd turn into the
understanding attorney and blow my act. By the time
we were together three months, I knew I'd never
want anyone but you. I couldn't wait to get home
and out of the movie rat race and into your arms.
You comforted me, soothed me, and I became an ad-
dict to your touch. I had turned into a family man
when I was supposed to be a swinger, and I didn't
care, because I had you."

Her mouth curved into a smile. "Then what took
you so long to realize my worth? I was certainly trying hard enough to bring it to your attention," she
said, her hand reaching up to touch the soft hair of
his sideburn. Her fingers crept around the strength of
his neck and cradled the back of his head, loving the
crisp, vibrant feel of his hair in the palm of her hand.

"You mean *that* was what you were trying to do
when you turned my underwear pink?" he teased,
and she blushed becomingly again. He chuckled and

gave a squeeze. "I was so busy trying to talk you into looking at me as the perfect love so you'd never leave me that I didn't realize you might have wants and needs, too. After I had softened you up enough, I was supposed to propose to you and you were supposed to swoon at my feet. It never dawned on me that you would turn me down." His smile slipped. "You scared the hell out of me. I didn't know what to do or where to go without you. Don't do that again, April. I don't know if I could take it."

His lips came down, tentatively at first, then with strength, as he sought an answer from her touch. His hands tightened on her hips, bringing her closer to him so that she could feel his need. She reveled in it.

All the manipulating she had tried, and she had never thought of telling him the truth! She should have let him know she wanted marriage. She had gone through this heartbreak for nothing. . . .

April pulled away to tell him of her deceptions, but the hungry look on his face told her he wouldn't care. He wanted her and that was all that mattered.

"Tomorrow we leave. Tonight we stay right here," he murmured, his eyes caressing her face, his thoughts apparent. "One of us is overdressed. Why don't you slip into something more comfortable? Like a scarlet heart? We could play that scene all over again, the way it was supposed to be, if you like."

"I like," she promised. "But where's Sid? Don't you think we owe it to him to feed him dinner? That was what he came for, wasn't it?"

Jace nodded. "He took your car back to his office. It'll be fine there until we're married. We can pick it up then." Suddenly he grinned, looking down at his unclothed body. "It feels a little awkward being the only one who's undressed. You don't think I'd dress this way if he were still wandering around, do you?"

She chuckled. "I should hope not! I'm the only person who can see you like this, Jace Sullivan, and don't you forget it!"

"I'm glad we agree. Now get undressed."

April's brows rose, but the mischief in her eyes belied her annoyance. "Issuing orders again, Jace?"

"Yes," he said unrepentantly. "Not that you'd obey them. I just like to keep my hand in so that the next time I have dealings with some starlet, I've not lost practice on telling her what she shouldn't do when I'm around."

"Like not to try to get you involved in publicity, and not to act the lover in public? Small, incidental things like that?"

"Right." His arms came up, pinning her to him as he slowly began dancing to soundless music. He edged his way down the hall and into the bedroom, humming off-key all the way.

April giggled. "It's a good thing you don't do musicals. We'd starve."

He laid her on the bed and stood looking down at her as he undid the snap of her cords. "Never sass a man with his belt off, lady. You could get in trouble."

"If it's the kind of trouble I have in mind, the belt will have to be on the floor, along with the rest of your clothes."

He joined her on the bed, his left arm circling to

hold her next to him as he slowly undid the buttons on her blouse with his right. His hands leisurely teased her flesh to tingles, his eyes showing the pleasure of unwrapping a gift at length.

"Jace?"

"Mmm?"

"I forgot. The studio telephoned. They want you to call back."

"It must be about the movie I want to do," he said absently as he pulled her blouse open enough to touch the sweet softness of her breasts.

"Which one?" April held her breath, but she couldn't say whether it was to hear the title or because of the miracle his hands were working.

"*Goodbye, Spring,*" he muttered. He bent down to taste one perked nipple. It was soft and sweet scented and fairly bloomed at the touch of his teasing lips. And it was just the right flavor: April Flynn flavor.

Her body went still. "Did you know your mother wants to play the female lead in it?" she asked quietly, waiting for him to back off and yell.

"Umm," he answered, lavishing attention on the other dusky peak. "Now shut up and let me love you."

"But—"

"I don't need to know whether they're going to back me. I'll call them later. As for my mother, we've made a sort of truce that might work well toward a peace." He gazed down at her. "But right now and for a long time to come, you're the most important thing in my world. So I repeat, shut up and let me love you."

"Yes, sir!" she whispered in his ear before gently nipping the lobe. Her arms wrapped around the hardness of his body, and she sighed contentedly.

"It's about time you learned your place, woman." His voice growled and she could feel the vibration of his words as her hand moved on his back.

"And just where is that? Certainly not in your bed, you chauvinist."

"No. Just where you are now. Next to me. For always, April soon-to-be-Sullivan." His voice was gruff with feeling, and his dark-brown eyes verified his love. "And April? Just for the record. I've never made love to, or even kissed another woman since you came into my life. Never," he said as if he had just made a vow.

"I know," she whispered, and she did. But just to make sure, she'd always be looking over his shoulder, ready to protect or fight for him.

His lips teased hers, never quite landing to give her the sustenance she craved, but something else niggled at her mind, not allowing her to fully enjoy his touch.

"Just one more thing," she said breathlessly as his hands searched her skin for those soft intimate places he knew so well. "Will you call your mother and tell her we're getting married? *Before* the news hits the gossip columns? Please?"

Jace raised his head, his eyes pouring love into her. "If it matters to you, I'll do it, but for no other reason, April," he murmured, kissing the tip of her nose. "I'll call her, and then I'm having that heart framed and hung in our bedroom. Maybe it will remind both of us what we really have. I love you, April. With all my heart." Then his lips hungrily covered hers to send shafts of delight coursing to her middle and radiating throughout her limbs.

April closed her eyes and let his kiss tell her the rest of his feelings. Someday, many years from now, when they were sitting in their rocking chairs on the back porch, she would recount the story of how she tried to make him propose. But for now, she thought it would be better for him not to be too arrogant and sure of her. After all, she still had to live with him for the next forty or fifty years. . . .

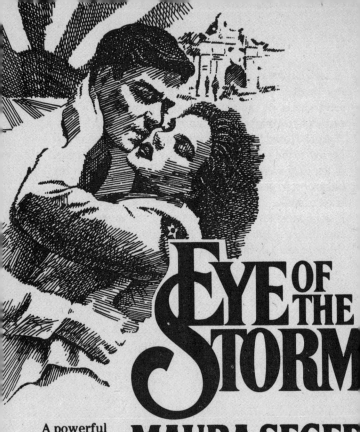

EYE OF THE STORM

MAURA SEGER

A powerful portrayal of the events of World War II in the Pacific, *Eye of the Storm* is a riveting story of how love triumphs over hatred. In this, the first of a three book chronicle, Army nurse Maggie Lawrence meets Marine Sgt. Anthony Gargano. Despite military regulations against fraternization, they resolve to face together whatever lies ahead.... Also known by her fans as Laurel Winslow, Sara Jennings, Anne MacNeil and Jenny Bates, Maura Seger, author of this searing novel was named by ROMANTIC TIMES as 1984's Most Versatile Romance Author.

At your favorite bookstore in March.